UNQUESTIONABLY MONSTROUS

By Alex Colvin

This collection is a work of fiction. All characters, locations, and events are the product of the author's imagination. Any references to historical events, real people, or locations are entirely fictionalized.

The views and opinions expressed in this collection are intended to be humorous and do not reflect the views and opinions of the author.

"I Hate Instant Mashed Potatoes" was originally published as "The Wrath of the Buttery Bastard Taters" in *MASHED: The Culinary Delights of Erotic Horror* by Grivante Press.

Dr. Reginald Fitzfauntleroy is entirely fictional and the quote on the front cover was written by the author.

Physical copy ISBN: 9798440972742

Also by Alex Colvin:

The Intellectual Barbarian

Forthcoming:

The Electric Heist

CONTENTS

Here There Be Monsters

Harold stepped into the dark gymnasium and looked around. The chairs were stacked by the far wall. Exactly where he'd left them. Perfect. Time to set everything up.

But first! Harold pulled his phone from his pocket, put his earbuds in, and put on a podcast. He was halfway through the latest episode of *Monstrous Conversations,* and he wanted to finish it before the meeting. He hit 'resume' and set to work.

"So, Dr. Fitzfauntleroy, would you say a general anti-monster sentiment is growing due to the ongoing zombie plague?"

"I... yes, but I should clarify that zombies are not actually considered monsters. The monster community disowns the actions of the zombie community and has no affiliation with them."

"Fascinating. Can you explain that?"

"Well, monsters are creatures with human intelligence but are supernatural in some way. They might be half-animal, invisible, immortal, or something considered unusual. Meanwhile, zombies are just people infected with ZBBV-23 who have lost all brain function except to hunt people down and eat them."

"And their population is growing, correct?"

"I'm not going to comment on that."

Harold snorted. Monsters ate people too. Hunted people. Tricked people. Monsters weren't much better than zombies, as far as Harold was concerned. He set the first chair down. Nine more to go. Or, wait... some people might skip the meeting due to the zombies. Nah. Probably not. Folks these days were lonely. Zombies hadn't been spotted in the area yet. Harold figured he'd better set up for a full house all the same. Harold pulled a second chair from the stack. He

1

carried it over to the centre of the gym. He turned away from his thoughts and back to the podcast.

"...That's an interesting point, but there are certain kinds of monsters who've been known to attack people. Did you hear about the werewolf attack at the furry convention this past—"

"That was just a misunderstanding. The werewolves apologized for—"

"I mean, they killed several people."

Yeah, Harold thought, you tell him. There was an uncomfortable pause in the podcast. Harold set the second plastic chair down. He looked at the chair. A single piece of hard plastic with four metal legs. Seemingly designed to be as uncomfortable as possible. Oh well. The meetings were only an hour. People could tolerate them for that long. He turned back for another one.

"Moving on. How would you recommend our listeners talk to their friends and family about achieving a monster-positive lifestyle?"

"That's an interesting question, Jordan. Being monster-positive, having monster friends, co-workers, or romantic partners, is an important step in social justice and global equality."

"Mm."

"Inviting monsters out to social events, being open to meeting monsters on dating apps, or connecting with them on social media can go a long way to forming bonds between the human and monster communities. The more people and monsters reach out to each other across, the more stereotypes and biases can be dispelled."

"Right. I mean, the stories of monsters eating, abducting, or seducing people are wildly exaggerated, right?"

"For the most part, yes."

Harold set down his chair and paused the podcast. These guys had no clue what they were talking about. Monsters were evil. Insane. Twisted. Harold had witnessed the cruelty of monsters firsthand. The very reason Harold was in the dark gymnasium, setting up chairs, was to create a safe space where the horrors of the world's monsters could be brought to light. Harold switched over to a better podcast and went back to setting up the last of the chairs.

The Death of a Mermaid

"You're not going to believe what I'm about to tell you."

"Josh, I've been a criminal lawyer for twenty years. I've heard it all."

"I think my girlfriend killed herself."

"Okay. We can talk about that, absolutely. But you *think* she killed herself? You're not certain?"

"I mean, she could still be alive. It's just, she swam out into the lake and disappeared three days ago. Around 4... maybe closer to 4:30."

"And you haven't seen her since?"

"No."

"Has her body washed up somewhere?"

"No."

"What's her name?"

"She... uh. She didn't have a name. There's, like, a gesture for it. But I have no idea what it sounds like. I couldn't write it down."

"I... what?"

"Okay. The thing is... she's... umm... a mermaid."

"A mermaid?"

"Yeah."

"In Lake Superior?"

"Yes. She was a mermaid, man. Don't look at me like that. I'm dead serious. Like, what do I do? Should I go to the cops?"

"She was seriously a mermaid? Like, living in the lake?"

"Yeah. We'd been living together for the past few weeks."

"What the fuck? Were you keeping her in your bathtub?"

"No! She grew legs before we met! She could breathe air!"

"What!?"

"Yeah, she grew legs, crawled out of the lake, and we hooked up!"

3

"Did you see her crawl out of the lake?"

"Yeah. She crawled onto my dock one night."

"Wow. Fuck."

"So, what do I do? Do I tell the police? Do you come with me?"

"No. God forbid. Talking to the police is the last thing you should do. Okay. First things first, I'm going to need a retainer fee."

"Uh. I guess that makes sense. How much?"

"Fifty grand."

"Fifty fucking grand? Are you kidding?"

"No, I am not kidding. If this girl's body washes up on someone's beach and she gets traced back to you and you're put on trial for murder, is your honest-to-God defence going to be, 'I'm pretty sure she was a mermaid and that she left me to rejoin the merpeople'?"

"No, she was seriously a mermaid. I know she was for a fact."

"Okay! Then explain this to me. From when she appeared to the night she went missing. Lay it out."

"Okay. So back in September? This woman crawls out of the lake when I'm out on my dock. Like, it's nine at night and I'm just having a drink. She climbs out and she's naked and freezing. She's got seaweed clinging to her skin and she's got twigs and shit in her hair. I brought her in because I thought she'd freeze to death if I didn't."

"Okay."

"And she just was out for three or four days, man. I put her in the guest bedroom right away with tons of blankets and stuff. I checked her temperature and tried to talk to her, to see if I could wake her up."

"Why didn't you take her right to the hospital?"

"I figured it would take them ages to get all the way out here. And maybe she was in some kind of trouble. Like, she didn't have any ID showing who she was. Maybe she escaped from something bad."

"Was she hot?"

"Oh, a total smokeshow. Just outrageously hot. I've got some pictures of her on my phone."

"Show me."

"Uh. Yeah... here you go."

"Oh. Wow. She's gorgeous."

"Like, easily the best-looking woman you've ever seen?"

"Yeah. But you should delete those pictures now that she's missing. Those are incriminating. You never showed them to me, got it?"

"Aww, seriously?"

"Yes. Take one last look and delete them. But she never had a tail?"

"No. She traded her tail for legs so we could be together."

"How'd she do that?"

"She was never *super* clear about that. From what I could gather, she made a deal with a magic crayfish or something to be human."

"Uh-huh. Did she show you anything to prove she was a mermaid?"

"Yeah. She had a necklace with a shell on it."

"Anything else?"

"What? Is that not good enough?"

"No, just curious. And what happened when she woke up?"

"She was cool. Tranquil. Peaceful and soothing to be around. She couldn't talk. She gestured at things. But we had a really nice time."

"Did you guys bang?"

"Oh, like, nonstop. Day and night. It was awesome."

"Nice."

"But, like, we tried to talk as well. She would draw me pictures of where she lived and of her family and stuff. She tried to teach me her mermaid sign language."

"How'd that go?"

"Okay. After a couple weeks we could communicate basic stuff."

"Okay... So what led to her... disappearance?"

"So, after a few weeks she got kind of moody and sad. Maybe she was homesick. So I tried to cheer her up and took her into town."

"You took her to Thunder Bay to cheer her up?"

"Yeah! What's wrong with that?"

"It's just... not a cheerful place. And, dude, there's a zombie pandemic going on. It's a two-hour drive to... the most depressing city in Canada."

"Yeah, but there's ice cream and sushi. I thought that would cheer her up."

"Did it?"

"No. She hated it. The city freaked her out entirely. All the cars and people and buildings. She was overwhelmed by it all and she signalled that she wanted to leave after we got something to eat. Once we got back to my cabin, she was just miserable."

"I see."

"And that afternoon she walked up to me, gave me a kiss, took her clothes off, and dove back into the lake. I watched her disappear and she never came up for air. I don't know if she drowned, or went back to her people, or what. But she's gone. I don't know what to do."

"Right. Well, I can help you there."

"And I miss her, dude. She was incredible."

"Uh, put a pin in that for a second. Not to take away from what you two had, but have you considered the possibility that she wasn't really a mermaid?"

"What?"

"Like, maybe she's crazy and told you all this because... reasons."

"You think she was lying?"

"I just wouldn't rule it out! She didn't bring over any mermaid friends to your place or anything. Maybe she's just some crazy homeless woman who does this for shits and kicks."

"Dude! How could you say that?"

"Look, she didn't have a tail. Or gills, right? She had a shell on a string and spoke in sign language? That's all the proof she had? Maybe she was just deaf and you're a fucking dumbass who didn't recognize sign language for what it was. Like, did she ever try to speak or anything?"

"No! It was mermaid sign language! And there was more to it than that! She seemed weirded out by breathing! She never caught on to the idea she could breathe with your mouth closed."

"So she was a mouth-breather? In that case, maybe she's just a crazy, horny, mentally-ill bitch who thinks she's a mermaid and does this whole routine for a place to crash for a few weeks. Or maybe–"

"I can't believe you! Mike, we've been friends for twenty years and you're saying you don't believe me?"

"I... mostly believe you! I legitimately believe that a hot girl climbed out of the lake, that you fucked like a couple of wild dolphins, and that she took off! But a mermaid? Seriously?"

"Dude, I am certain she was a mermaid. There's other proof."

"Such as?"

"She fucking loved sushi."

"She's a white girl! That's how they're wired! Doesn't mean shit."

"She would dive down to the lake and collect sea glass and fossils! She had a collection she kept on my desk."

"My wife loves collecting shiny shit too! And she's not a mermaid. Hell, she can barely swim."

"I'm telling you; she was a mermaid. Like, she was insanely critical of *The Little Mermaid* and pointed out everything that was inaccurate in that movie. It was annoying as hell."

"Okay, okay. Fine."

"So, what do I do?"

"Go on a trip. Is there anywhere you've ever wanted to go?"

"Uh. Yeah. I've always wanted to see the Yukon. You know, see the wilderness and where the gold rush happened."

"Perfect. Go there for six months."

"Six months?!"

"I mean, six months minimum. A year or two would be ideal."

"I have to pay you fifty grand *and* go live in the wilderness for a year? What the fuck? You're supposed to help me!"

"Do you have any idea what a nightmare of a case this is? What an absolute shitshow this would be if it went to trial? Like, mermaids aren't people. She doesn't technically have Canadian citizenship or human rights. But that could be wide open to debate. Plus, Lake Superior borders Canada and the United States. She could be from the American side of the fucking lake for all we know. Or she could wash up over there. Your 'mermaid' could become an international dispute. As a fucking bonus, there is no legal precedent for defending against a crime committed against a 'mermaid'. This monster shit is still new. It'll require an absolute shitload of research. That's why the retainer fee is so high."

"Okay..."

"Like, you do not have a leg to stand on if this were to become a jury trial. Because you can either: a) tell the jury with a straight face that you were fucking a mermaid, which not everyone believes in, and when she swam off you figured she was just rejoining her people, or

b) she was some mute, or mentally-ill, abuse victim, who stayed with you, who you didn't take to the authorities for whatever reason, and that you were so devastated by her disappearance that you went into a deep depression and didn't call the cops. Neither looks good on you."

"Okay..."

"So get the hell out of Dodge. Go to the Yukon or something until either her body washes up and the investigation is over, or there's this community drive to find this missing girl that eventually peters out, or nothing comes of it. Either way, leave town until the world forgets or never finds out about her."

"In cop shows, the police always warn people not to leave town after these kinds of things happen."

"Yeah, because the police really like having a suspect and knowing where their suspect is. Makes their jobs easier. If the public freaks out about her washing up, the cops can just pin everything on you."

"Oh. Oh shit."

"Yeah. Go to the Yukon. I'll take care of this."

"But... if I'm in the Yukon..."

"Yeah?"

"What if she comes back? What if she comes home and I'm not there?"

"Uh..."

"Mike, I'm sorry, but what she and I have is too special. I can't leave. She might come back. Maybe she met up with the crayfish and is a mermaid again. What if she's still alive? We had a connection."

"Uh-huh. Did you guys use protection at all?"

"Um. No."

"And she wasn't on any mermaid birth control or anything?"

"No, I don't think so."

"Well, maybe you're dodging a bullet here. If I were you, I'd count my blessings and run like Hell. Meet a girl who was born on dry land. Or on a boat. Just not underwater."

"But what if she comes back for me?"

"You said she collects shiny shit from the bottom of the lake?"

"Yeah."

"Draw her a picture. It doesn't have to be art, just draw her something so she knows you're away and that you'll be back. Put it in a bottle with some sand and throw it in. If she comes back for you, she might see it. She can read it. She'll know you're coming home."

"So... you do believe me."

"Sorry?"

"You know she's a mermaid! You know it! You just told me how to win her back! Like how to contact an actual mermaid."

"I'm just helping a friend. And now, I'm changing gears and I'm protecting a client. Delete those pictures off your phone. Make sure there's nothing on the Cloud. Wipe your ConnectPage or ClickSnap, or whatever. Clean your house like your life depends on it. But your plane tickets with cash. Pack a suitcase. Get out of here by tomorrow."

"Okay. What are you going to do?"

"Read case law. I've got to come up with something in case she shows up. I've got to go. I'll call you tomorrow."

"Thanks, man."

"Any time. Also, I gotta say, you're remarkably composed about all this. I'm impressed."

"Oh, no, not really. I'm just insanely high right now. I have been since she vanished."

"What?!"

"Yeah, man. It's the only way I can keep calm. I'm worried that if I come down, I'll start sobbing. So I'm keeping a buzz on."

"Well, you're going to have to come down eventually."

"Shit, you're right. Dude. Whenever that happens, I'll probably cry like a baby."

Sex Demon

"Are you ready for this man? This is going to be the greatest night of our lives."

"Oh yeah, bro. This is going to be epic. Historic. Legendary. Let's do this."

Tyler and I were preparing to summon a succubus. A sex demon from the depths of Hell who would have wild, insane sex with us until we were close to death. We had everything just about ready to summon her, and we were fucking pumped.

The whole thing had honestly come about on a fluke. I'd been working on an essay in the Sheaffe University library. Sick of looking at my computer screen, I glanced at the nearby bookshelves and an ancient book caught my eye. It was bound in leather, filled with handwritten script was on parchment paper. There was no title and no author. But the book contained ancient spells. Dark magic. Spells to summon plagues, destroy crops, obliterate empires, and even far more sinister things deeper in the volume. Dreary shit, man. I was about to put it back on the shelf when I found the spell to summon a succubus. That spell convinced me to check the book out of the library and show it to my Tyler. It was an easy spell, and as soon as Tyler had read it over, he said, "We have to try this one."

"I agree. We'll need to pick up a few things."

"Let's go right now. We can take my truck."

"Deal."

Off we went. We picked up some red watercolour paint, some candles, and a bottle of wine.

Like I said, the spell wasn't hard to set up. We had to light eight candles and place them in a circle on the floor. Within the circle of candles, Tyler drew a summoning symbol in red. It can be ink, blood, paint, whatever, but it has to be red. I suggested watercolour paint so we could wash it off after, no problem. We also had to leave a glass of red wine at the edge of the circle as an offering to the succubus. The spell book said that once she arrived, she would sip the wine and we would have to offer her the rest of the bottle. No problem. Then she was ours until sunrise. Fuck yeah. After fifteen minutes of prep, we had everything ready to go.

Which brings us to now. Tyler and I were standing in front of the summoning circle. I nodded at him, and he gave a single nod back. I opened the ancient tome and read the summoning incantation:

"O magne vir post velum;
Succubum affer in mundum!
Sic fera nox feroces sexus;
Et mater mea hunc librum claudet in aeternum.

For a moment, everything was still and calm.

Then everything went black. The lights, the candles, even the streetlights outside, were extinguished. All light seemed to vanish from the universe. There was a brilliant flash of red light and a moment of agonizing heat as a portal to Hell opened. For the single moment the portal was open, an ungodly chorus of tortured screams and cries for mercy roared from the portal. They ceased the next instant. The lights began to shine once again, and the succubus was standing in the middle of the summoning circle.

She was not what Tyler and I had been expecting.

She looked to be in her mid-70s. She was stooped and hunched. Rotund, but with skinny arms and legs. Her hair was a faded, unsettling shade of purple and was piled on her head in a haphazard beehive. Her hair did not, however, obscure the wickedly-sharp horns that grew out of her forehead. But that was the only demonic thing about her. She was jowly, and her nicotine-stained fingers were holding a cigarette up to her thin lips. Her hand fell to her side and she exhaled a cloud of noxious smoke. "Hey there, honey," she said in a voice that had been sanded down to a gravelly rasp. "Thanks for the call."

11

Uh oh. Tyler and I exchanged nervous glances. Were we obliged to have sex with her? I mean, we'd summoned her. If we just called this whole thing off, would she curse us or flay us alive? And what the hell had gone wrong? We were expecting someone young and hot. Tyler was the braver of the two of us and ventured a question, "Uh, hi. Are you the succubus?"

"That's me, honey. What is it you boys are looking for? Blowjobs? Handjobs? Something with feet? I've done it all, and I'm up for whatever," she took a drag of her cigarette. "Do you want to do this here, or in a bedroom, or what?"

"Are you sure you want to do this?" I asked. Tyler nodded encouragingly. "I mean, we summoned you, but are you here against your will? We—" I glanced over at Tyler, whose nodding grew more vigorous by the second, "—don't want to do anything if you were forced to come here. We can call this whole thing off."

The succubus took another generous hit of her cigarette. "No, honey. We're not forced to come to these things. Whenever there's a summoning order, we all get the notification and anyone can accept the gig. I was the only one who wanted it, so here I am."

She picked up the wine and took a sip. She grimaced but managed to swallow it. "This is some really cheap shit, honey." She dropped her cigarette butt in the wine, extinguishing it.

"Why are you the only succubus who answered our summon? Like, we weren't competitive?" I asked. "Like, no one else wanted to come party with us?"

"Nope. Just me."

"Why is that?" Tyler asked. "We're young. We're hot. We work out. This was set to be a wild night."

The succubus said nothing and gave our apartment a once-over. "You boys want an honest answer?"

"Yes," Tyler and I said in unison.

"Look around this place and tell me what you see."

I glanced around the living room of the apartment. My home. My... oh. Wait. Maybe she had a point. The coffee table was covered with beer cans, old bottles, and plates with bits of food on them. The table was very sticky and some of the cans and bottles were probably stuck there permanently. There was a pile of soggy pizza boxes in the

12

corner I hadn't gotten around to throwing out yet. Clothes were strewn around. There were open DVD and Xbox cases all around the TV, with disks scattered around them like the wreckage of a plane crash. God knows if there was a single disk in the right case. Tyler's textbooks and notes were in a heap on the couch, which I referred to as his nest. And that was just the living room. Most of our kitchen appliances looked like they'd been deep-fried and even Tyler and I agreed the bathrooms were getting gross. "This place could use some cleaning," Tyler finally said.

"This place is a fucking dump," the succubus agreed. "I mean, look around. And this wine is absolute shit. It tastes like grape juice mixed with battery acid and piss. Tell me honestly, honey, where did you get it? What made you choose it?"

"It was the cheapest thing at the grocery store," I said, defeated. "I didn't want to spend more than ten bucks."

"And that," she said. "Is why you ended up with me. No young demon with any self-respect would set foot in here. But I figured, what the hell, I could use a night out. But if you want to get a hot young thing in here, you boys need to put the work in."

She hobbled over to Tyler's recliner. She swept the LEGO, pencils, and cookie crumbs from the seat. She sat down with a groan. "I'll make you boys a deal," she said. "You got anything else to drink around here?"

"I've got a bottle of whisky," Taylor said. "Why?"

"Bring me the bottle, get me an ashtray, and turn on the radio. I'll just help myself and tell you boys what to do. Once things are straightened out, you can try the summoning ritual again and I guarantee you'll get an absolute knockout. Deal?"

"Deal," I said, before Tyler could try to haggle. It was his whisky she was going to be downing, after all. But I'd square up with him after.

"Alright. Get some bowls or buckets and fill them with soapy water. Find some garbage bags. And get me that whisky. We'll turn things around faster than you think."

I went into the kitchen to do her bidding, and Tyler followed. Once we were out of the succubus's sight, Tyler turned to me. "Dude, what the Hell?"

13

"What?"

"You're going to let her drink all my booze and make us clean the apartment? This is bullshit! Let's tell her to get going and we'll make a new plan! Just make her go back to Hell. Yeah, let's do that and go meet some human girls who don't give a shit that we're dirty. They're way hotter than this old bag we summoned!"

"Come on, man! We gotta do this! We know the ritual works! We just gotta class it up. Yeah, sure, we can go meet some college girls. Or we can fuck an actual demon who is specifically designed for sex. Seemingly for free. Right?"

"I... I think so. Did the book not say if there was a fee?"

"No. It was just the spell. Maybe she gets our data or something."

"Oh, no big deal then."

"We just need to put the work in. It'll be worth it."

Tyler scowled. "It'd better be. And you're paying me back for that whisky."

"Deal."

We filled a bucket and a Tupperware container with soapy water and grabbed some rags. Tyler dug out a roll of garbage bags from under the sink. I got the whisky. We returned to the succubus for further instructions. "Okay, boys. Throw out all the garbage and scrub everything. Start at the highest places you can reach, and work your way down. Always clean with gravity. Get to it."

We did as she commanded. Tyler peeled the bottles and beer cans off the table and got to work on the mountain of pizza boxes. I got to cleaning and scrubbing every cleared surface. The succubus took hits of the whisky straight from the bottle and burned through another cigarette. I felt kind of sorry for her, and I hoped she wasn't too let down by how the evening was going. "Sorry that we're not, you know, getting to stuff and that we dragged you out here for nothing," I said to her as I made progress on the coffee table. "I hope you're not too disappointed. Um, are we supposed to pay you or something?"

"Oh, not at all, honey. And normally you'd pay with your souls, but you don't have to pay if we don't screw. But even if I don't get paid, I'm just glad to have a night out. And it's been a long time since I've bossed two young men around." She gave me a wink.

Okay then.

An hour later, the apartment was presentable. All garbage and junk had been hauled away, and every surface had been either washed, swept, or vacuumed. Things had been put away, organized, and straightened out. Tyler and I approached the succubus, who was down to half a bottle. "Good stuff, boys. Now you gotta smarten yourselves up."

"What's wrong with how we're dressed?" Tyler asked.

The succubus just stared at him and said nothing. He was wearing flip-flops, a stained wife-beater, and shorts. I didn't look much better in a ratty old t-shirt and a pair of boxers. "Either of you own shirts with collars? Pants that reach your feet? Or shoes that are one solid colour?"

"I do," I said. "And I can lend Tyler some."

She nodded. "Do that. And one of you go get some nicer wine. Spend at least twenty bucks."

"Twenty bucks? That's more than I earn in an hour! On wine?"

"Then find a better job, honey. Don't cheap out on the wine. Fine women like fine drink. It'll be worth every penny."

A grumbling and grumpy Tyler left to go get nicer wine. "Something French," the succubus suggested.

I put on an outfit I usually reserve for going to the bar and put my backup on Tyler's bed. Once he was back (he went beyond expectations and got a twenty-two-dollar bottle of French wine) and changed, we went back to our summoning circle, and poured a fresh glass of the new wine. Tyler and I, looking rather dapper, if I do say so myself, approached the circle once again. We were going to get a fucking sexy one this time. I could feel it. I opened the ancient book and read the summoning spell. The lights went out, the portal to hell opened once again. Once the portal closed, a new succubus was standing in the middle of the summoning circle.

She was painfully beautiful.

She was tall with long chestnut-coloured hair and blue eyes. Her playful smile revealed a set of perfect, if slightly pointy, teeth. She had delicate hands, long legs, and a figure that struck an impossible balance of voluptuous and innocent. She also had horns, but they were easy to ignore with everything else she had going on. The elderly succubus glanced over at her. "Hey, Maeve."

UNQUESTIONABLY MONSTROUS

"Evening Gracie," Maeve said, before turning to the glass of wine at the edge of the summoning circle. She bent over and picked up the glass. She took a sip and smiled. "Would you like the rest of the wine?" I asked.

"I would."

She took a delicate step out of the summoning circle and looked Tyler and I over. She smiled again. "Hello boys."

"Oh yeah, this is it!" Tyler did a fist-pump. Without another word, he started tearing his clothes off. Once he was naked, he gave the new succubus a nod. "Let's do this. You can start by going down on me. Here is fine, but the shower and my bedroom are also options."

Maeve's smile dissolved into a look of disdain. "Excuse me?"

"You're a sex demon, right? Let's have some sex!"

Maeve took a step back and was now standing within the summoning circle. "Just like that? Like I'm some kind of servant you can boss around? God, your souls aren't worth shit. I mean, you two won't even ask me how my day was or if you can get me anything else?"

"Oh, wait," I said. "Yes, we can absolutely do that."

"Oh, come on!" Tyler said. "This has already been an ordeal! We had to do all kinds of shit just to get you here! So are you gonna bang us, or what?"

Maeve rolled her eyes. "How about you dickheads jerk each other off? Spare Gracie, please. I can do so much better than this. Bye."

The second succubus vanished in a puff of smoke. Tyler let out a shriek of dismay, falling to his knees. I just stood there, speechless. "Oh yeah," our elderly succubus said. "You always gotta treat them like a lady. Even if they're just here to get some dick. I guess I should have told you boys that, but I thought it was a given."

I sat down on the sofa, totally defeated. Tyler sat down next to me, his head in his hands. Our succubus polished off the last of the whisky and lit a fresh cigarette. "You know, boys," she said. "My offer for blowjobs and handjobs still stands. Either of you interested?"

Tyler and I just looked at each other. Neither of us spoke.

An Okay Cupid

I scanned the restaurant and looked over my options. There were two guys in a dark corner having a highly engaged conversation. They couldn't look away from each other and were both listening and speaking with great care and affection. I nocked an arrow just in case they were gay. I flew a little closer to hear what they were saying:

"I'm telling you, there's no such thing as postmodernism. It's just modernism pushed to its logical conclusion."

"But how do you explain the total lack of conventions in contemporary writing if it isn't a new movement entirely?"

Oh god. Not gay. Never mind. Just graduate students. Forget it. They're on their own.

I spotted another couple. A guy with glasses and a woman in a knit cap. They looked super awkward. Probably an early date. Putting an arrow in either of them could be a disaster. I skipped them.

The third table looked promising. Maybe a third or fourth date. Natural conversation. A woman with a dazzling smile and a hipster-looking dude. He was telling a story and she was laughing. Genuine laughter. They had chemistry. "No, I'm serious," he said. "I legitimately thought the words to 'Livin' La Vida Loca' were 'Lips like devilled eggs/skin like Karla Homolka'. Like, until last year."

"You did not!"

"Yeah, I figured Ricky Martin was trying to say this girl had really soft lips and, I dunno, maybe Karla Homolka has nice skin. Like, I grew up around where Paul Bernardo... um... killed people. And people around there used to talk about how they were good-looking. I thought maybe that got back to Ricky and he was being super edgy. I was super young, in my defence."

The girl laughed. The hipster dude grinned sheepishly. Oh yeah, this was solid gold. I nocked an arrow and took aim. I waited for them to look into each others' eyes, and I took my shot. I caught the hipster dude in the back of the head, and before it could register, I fired a second shot and hit the girl in the neck. They both twitched. Then they both gave huge, unabashed smiles that lit up their faces. They leaned in closer and began talking intently. The hipster dude took the woman's hand, which she'd left out on the table for him. It was a lovely sight. They left the café a few minutes later. Have fun, kids.

But. It didn't mean anything yet. Cupid work, you may be surprised to learn, is commission based and we only get paid out on relationships that 'go firm', i.e. they get married. So it can take months or even years to get paid out for a successful shot. Not like in the old days when people got married right away. Plus, cupid arrows wear off eventually, and these days, most of my arrows go to waste. My meagre savings weren't going anywhere and retirement was looking less likely each century. My mood soured as I considered all of this, and I was fuming by the time I was set to take my smoke break.

At 8 pm, I flew over to a billboard near the railway tracks. Kalliope, a blond cupid with a winning smile and adorable dimples, was already sitting on the billboard ledge, waiting for me, and digging into a box of chocolates. "Hey Calisto," she said through a mouthful of chocolate and fruit filling. "Good night so far?"

"Some decent shots," I landed on the ledge with a thump. "Looked like a few would turn into romances. Hopefully money in the bank. You?"

Kalliope shrugged. "Four or five shots tonight. Two that looked really promising."

I lit a cigarette and inhaled. My mood was vile, but smoking wasn't taking the edge off. Kalliope seemed to sense danger, and gave me room to maneuver. "Anything on your mind?"

"I mean, other than how bullshit the pay is?"

"Yeah, anything else bothering you?"

Yes, actually. Centuries of frustration boiled over and I began to rant. "I'm just sick of this job. Why are we still using arrows after four-thousand years? Why can't we use paintball guns? Or sniper rifles? That could save us from all the flying around. We're just living, breathing drones that deliver love. Half the time, the effort is for nothing. We're getting completely fucked by Tinder. No pun intended. Management just insists on doing things the way they always have, and it sucks. It's always sucked but it especially sucks now that there are so many options and different ways to do things. And you never know if you're actually getting paid for your work. And it feels so empty and meaningless... I'm just... done. But what else can I even do? I've only got one goddamn skill that's worth anything," I gestured at the bow that was lying next to me. "So I'm... stuck. And I hate that."

Kalliope gave her remaining chocolates a calculating look and decided she could spare a couple. She offered me the box. I took one and chewed glumly. She inched closer to me, "Maybe you need a break? Some time off?"

"I don't get paid for time off. Gig work. Ugh."

Kalliope patted me on the shoulder. "I know. It's a grind. Have you ever thought about going commercial?"

Huh? I turned and looked over at her. She was smiling, her famous dimples lightening my mood more than my cigarette did. She was also serious. What was she talking about? "Commercial?"

"Sure! A commercial cupid! I know a couple of us who've been hired by Electric City and Pomegranate."

"Doing what?"

"Shooting people with arrows, silly! I mean, our arrows make people fall in love with whatever they're looking at. It doesn't have to be a person. If they're looking at a phone, or a pair of headphones, or a TV, it'll still work. I mean, you could work at an animal shelter. I work there sometimes, just for the joy of it. But plenty of cupids get burnt out on the love game and go into sales."

I perked up. I mean, it sounded a bit immoral, but like easy money! "How do you find a gig like this?"

"Just drop off a résumé! Most big stores have a cupid department. Just go in and introduce yourself."

"Wow!" My spirits lifted. A way out. Yes. "Thank you so much!"

Kalliope looked pleased. She loves playing matchmaker, which is why she's been happy to be a love cupid for thousands of years.

Matching me up with a new job must have counted. "You're welcome! And feel free to use me as a reference."

"You're the best! I'll stop by Electric City tomorrow!"

***

The next morning, I flew over to the nearest Electric City. I hovered outside the door, suddenly nervous. I hadn't started a new job in thousands of years. I hadn't been the new guy in forever. Maybe my job was actually okay... but then I thought about doing another miserable shift of shooting people in half-empty movie theatres and bars, not knowing what relationships would go firm and which ones I'd get paid for. The hell with that. On to something new.

I flew in the front door and looked around. Trying to talk to a human employee would be a waste of time, they can't see cupids. But I didn't see any cupids working anywhere. I wondered if Kalliope had made some kind of mistake. I turned to leave and bumped into a cupid who'd been hovering behind me. He grunted, and I took a few flaps backward. "Oh! Sorry, man!" I said.

"Whatever," he said. He was a heavyset cupid, with coke bottle glasses, and a five-o'clock shadow. He was wearing an Electric City uniform. "You here for work?"

"Uh, yeah. Do you want a copy of my résumé? Or should we do an interview?"

"What? No. You can start now. You have your bow and arrow?"

"Oh. Um. On me? No."

"Doesn't matter, you can borrow one for now. Follow me."

We flew up to a cupid-sized door near the ceiling, labelled "PRODUCT RELATIONSHIP COORDINATOR", and I followed him inside. I found myself in a sparse office with a couple of desks and a wall of bows and quivers. "By the way," the boss cupid said, "name's Oulixes. You'll report all your shots to me and I'll sort your commission payments. They will be compared to our sales logs. So do not fuck with me. Okay? If you do, I'll know, and that's it. You pick your shifts and you get paid at the end of each workday. Questions?"

"Yeah. The pay is commission-based?"

"That's right. You get 15% of all items you encourage customers to buy. That sound good to you?"

Shit, yeah! I looked out the small office window and surveyed the store. Some of those laptops were well over a grand. Large appliances could easily fetch two or three. Not to mention phones, tablets, drones, and watches. Fifteen percent on any of this stuff would make me richer than sin in a week! My new boss handed me a bow and a quiver full of arrows. "You know how to get a clean shot?" he asked.

"Yeah. Only shoot when you see a serious connection. Some kind of spark or attraction. Otherwise, it'll wear off and make a mess." I shouldered the quiver and tested out the bow. It wasn't great, but I could work with it. "I've been doing this with people for ages, how do you know if someone has that kind of connection to a watch or a dishwasher?"

"Because they look longingly at it. Read their faces, just like the love game. Also, any returned items come out of your next payday, so don't try to force anything," Oulixes said. "If you're any good, you'll do well. It's that simple. Now get out there and sell some shit."

I did a couple of circles around the store, getting a sense of the layout. On my second pass, I noticed this balding guy in jeans and a t-shirt. He was looking longingly at a pair of $500 noise-cancelling Bluetooth headphones. He poked at the ear coverings. He tried them on and a blissful look crossed his face as he listened to whatever muzak was playing. He took them off, but continued to stare at them. I nocked an arrow. But, I thought, maybe he has a good reason not to go for it. Maybe he doesn't have the money. Maybe in his heart of hearts, he knows it won't make him happy.

Ah, fuck it. I mean, it was his choice to come into the store, right?

I let loose my arrow and hit him square in the middle of his back. The effect was instantaneous.

"Oh, fuck yes!" he cried, holding the headphones above his head, gazing up at them like they were a sacred religious artifact. "These will complete me! These will make me whole again! Make me a man again! You're coming home with me!"

The balding guy sprinted to checkout, headphones in hand. "I'll take one of these!"

"Okay," the checkout person said. "Visa or debit card?"

"Visa!"

And that was that. Once the guy had his new headphones, he danced out of the store and I swear to God he clicked his heels in the parking lot on his way to the car.

"Congrats, kid. You just made sixty bucks."

I turned around and saw Oulixes hovering behind me. He was grinning. "See? Nothing to it. Look for a personal attachment, and shoot. You'll walk out of here with six-hundred bucks a day, easy. Let me know if anything comes up."

I circled the store. I found another guy, a businessman-type in an expensive suit with coiffed hair. He was taking a long look at a retro, 1950's style toaster. Bingo. I shot him from across the store and caught him in the side of his head. He shuddered, and then lunged for the toaster. He moaned once the toaster was wrapped in his arms. "You're coming home with Daddy," he said. "You're all mine, baby."

He ran to the counter in a frenzy. The checkout person looked a touch nervous. "Can I help you?"

"Yes, I'm taking this toaster home. This exact one. Right now."

"Absolutely," she said, sensing this man was not in his right mind and speaking gently. "Would you like to pay with credit or debit? Would you like me to put it in a bag?"

"No!" the man cried, clutching it to his chest. "No one! And I mean not a soul other than myself, will ever touch this toaster again! She will be my wife, my whore, my matron, my concubine, my angel, and my muse! I will break your hands if you try to touch her."

The saleswoman nodded. "Sure thing."

He paid with an American Express card and escaped the store, snarling like a wounded animal. He was out of the store in less than a minute, running off to his car to... oh, who knows. I have to admit, I wasn't feeling too pleased with myself while I watched this spectacle unfold. I might have even looked a little queasy, because Oulixes flew over and gave me a nod. "You okay, rookie?"

"That was really bizarre."

Oulixes shrugged. "Some people are sick fucks. Haven't you seen stuff like that from your romance cupid days?"

"Oh yeah, some people just bang right then and there when you shoot them. But never, you know, a dude and a toaster."

"It's more common than you think. But you're doing good, kid. Get back out there and make your fortune!"

"Thanks, boss."

***

"You got the job?"

"I got the job!"

"Oh, Calisto!" Kalliope leaned over and gave me a hug. "That's wonderful! I'll think you'll do great."

"Thanks!" I presented my thank-you gift to her, an elegant box of chocolates. Her eyes went wide and she dug into them straight away. "They seem happy to take on any new cupids who want the work," I said. "Do you want in on this? I can mention you."

"Oh no," she said. "I like the love game. I always like to think about how many people I've helped fall in love. And how many people are here today because of me. I can't give it up."

"Suit yourself," I said. "But feel free to stop by my work sometime. You can see what the scoop is."

"It's a date!"

***

Two weeks went by. I worked three or four shifts a week and made people fall in love with tablets, TVs, cameras, and a couple of treadmills. The cash poured in. I mean, I had more money in the bank than ever before. I was considering my first vacation in a hundred years. Things were good. Oulixes was pleased with me. "Kid, you beat my expectations. You're a natural at this. If you want to stick this out, you can go all the way to the top. Trust me on this."

I didn't know what "all the way to the top" meant for Electric City, but I liked the sound of that. Over the next month, I picked up extra shifts, and I worked busy days. Things were good.

One cool April night, there was a guy waiting for me by the main door to Electric City at the end of my shift. He was a cupid, and he was wearing a beautifully tailored Armani suit made from virgin wool, with a silk shirt. He was leaning against the wall, smoking a cigar. His shoes are gleaming in the streetlight. He gave me a winning smile. "You must be the new guy I keep hearing about. I hear you're hot shit, kid."

"Uh, thanks," I said. "Who are you?"

"The name's Cassander. But that's not important. The real question is, how much did you earn tonight? Seven hundred? Eight?"

"One thousand, two hundred."

I don't know why I told him, but there you go. Maybe it was his clothes. Maybe it was his casual confidence. It made me want to show him up. His smile widened. "That's a good number. But still minor league. Have a drink with me. I'd like to talk to you about a job."

"Thanks, but I really like my job."

"Just let me buy you a drink, kid. And something to eat. Anything you want. You can hear me out and we'll run the numbers on what you could be earning. You can say yes or no, but I have a feeling you'll say yes."

I mean, who says no to a free meal? "Alright. Where are we going?"

"I know a good place."

The 'good place' turned out to be the single most expensive restaurant in town. It had a special cupid section with smaller furniture and cupid wait staff. I had no idea it even existed. They all seemed to know who Cassander was. They treated him like a general. His 'usual table' was ready in less then a minute. A cupid hostess seated us in a cavernous dining room, festooned with lights in little bubbles that make the ceiling look like our own personal galaxy.

I took my seat, and it struck me that I'd never sat in such a comfortable chair. It was soft, yet firm, and perfectly balanced. I could sit in it forever. I faced Cassander across an oak table, laden with a baffling amount of silverware and glassware. A waiter flew over to us the moment I settled into my seat. "Good evening," she said, offering a dazzling smile. "Can I start you off with a couple of drinks?"

"A Manhattan for me," Cassander said. "And a martini for my guest. The moment his glass is empty, bring him another one."

The waitress took off. Cassander grinned. "What do you think, kid?"

"This is amazing."

"It's fine. It doesn't hold a candle to some places in Japan or Paris. If we go into business together, I'll take you to this one place in Japan that literally only has one table. The chef there is terrific. You get this twenty-course meal that's just life-changing. But, you know, this place is pretty good for where it is."

"And what is it that you do?"

Cassander's grin widened. Our drinks were brought over, and he took a sip of his Manhattan. "I'm in finance. I work for a bank."

"Doing what?" I asked, sipping my own drink. My God. It was extraordinary. I didn't know martinis could even taste like that. Damn.

"Recruiting cupids," he said. "Best job in the world. I look for talent and bring them in. And you, kid, are liquid talent. You're merciless. You sell shitloads of product. You're the kind of cupid we need."

Between the martini and the high praise, I was feeling like royalty. "Doing what?" I asked. "Sales?"

"Exactly. Selling the bank's services to existing clients."

Wait... was that logical? Another martini had been set in front of me and I'd already made good progress on it. "Wait, why do existing clients need the bank's services?"

Cassander gave me an approving look. "Ah, got a smart one here. Interesting. Look, our clients just don't realize the full extent of what the bank can offer them. They think we can just hold their money for them. But we can do so, so much more. Investments. Retirement plans. Mortgages. Second mortgages. High-interest savings accounts. Overdraft protection. Lines of credit. Loans. And you, my friend, you can help people see the value in these services."

"Yeah?"

"Of course! When our customer service representatives mention these services and show our clients our pamphlets, that's the perfect time to shoot them! That way, they can see past their biases or shyness and sign up for services that will hugely benefit them!"

My brain was drowning in martinis, and a third, or maybe even a fourth one had just been set in front of me. "And these services help people?"

"Oh, 100%! A generous overdraft can be the difference between seeing the dentist or not for some people! Or getting your car to the shop over hoping it doesn't just break down on them! Trust me, you're saving lives. Oh, and you get $1,000 for every shot that leads to a sign-up for a new service."

Fuck. So if I managed five shots a day, that's $5,000. And if I work four days a week... fifty weeks a year... how much money was that? The numbers danced around my mind, refusing to line up and let me make any calculations. But, I decided, the calculations were moot. It was a lot of money. I didn't need any stupid math to tell me that. "I'm in," I said. "Tell me where to shoot and I'll do it."

Cassander laughed, and we shook on it. "Be at the bank tomorrow morning. Kid, this is the first day of a glorious new life for you. You're going to have to see it to believe it."

I zig-zagged back to my apartment, nearly colliding with a few streetlights and I had one near-miss with a tree. I collapsed into bed, the world spinning around me, thinking about the gigantic house I would buy once I had some dough saved up. Not just gigantic by cupid standards. I would buy a huge house even by mortal standards. It would be my castle, and I would be king.

***

My brain felt like it was trying out power tools on my skull the next morning, but I still flew to work with a spring in my flap. Cassander was waiting for me outside the bank, in a different but equally expensive suit, a grin plastered all over his face. "Alright kid! This is a cakewalk! Wait for our representative to show the client the pamphlet, and shoot the client! They almost always sign up for the new service, and you pocket a shitload of cash! Take breaks whenever you want, and you can go home after ten shots. Or you can hang around as long as you want! I don't give a fuck. See ya!"

To illustrate his indifference, Cassander lit a cigar and flew off to sunbathe on the roof of a nearby building. I'd later learn he had a recliner and a minifridge up there. He didn't share the contents of the minifridge with anyone. But from the first second of my first day, I was on my own. I flew into the bank and hovered around the ceiling, waiting for a client to show up.

An older gentleman in a gleaming suit stepped into the bank. He approached the teller. "I need to transfer $10,000 to my daughter's account. For school tuition. For... summer school."

Yeah, sure thing pal. But the teller didn't bat an eye. I would have bet my newfound job that he had no children to speak of, but the teller just smiled and nodded. I got an arrow ready. "And would you like to hear about our new overdraft and line of credit options for existing customers?" she asked.

Twang. "No, I... oh. Oh! Yes please! Absolutely!"

The teller nodded. "Wonderful, sign here, sir."

Yee-haw! Money in the bank!

But, little did I know, a storm was brewing. Remember how I said to Kalliope that she could stop by my work someday? Well, she went to Electric City to look for me, and I wasn't there. She asked Oulixes where I was, and he told her I'd moved on to work at the bank down the street. She flew into the bank, just in time to see me shooting a middle-aged man who was looking at a pamphlet about a $40,000 line of credit. He signed up for the line of credit, additional overdrafts, and a new high-interest savings account. Cha-ching! My target danced out of the store, shouting, "Wow! $40,000 in free money! I'm getting another car!"

Kalliope's expression grew stony as she watched my target leave. I noticed her for the first time, and waved. "Look who it is!" I said. "Welcome to the big show!"

"What the hell are you doing?"

"Convincing people to sign up for lines of credit and overdrafts. Why?"

In my thousands of years of experience with romance, I have learned that there can be wrong answers when it comes to women's questions. A secondary lesson is that, sometimes, totally logical and straightforwardly honest answers are also the wrong ones. I realized the moment I spoke that I had given a 'wrong' answer. Kalliope's plump, unfailingly cheerful face was now a stony mask of fury. She tightened her grip on her bow. "What?" she growled.

"Uh... you know. That's my job at the bank. I shoot people when they're told about the bank's services so they'll sign up for them. The pay is off the charts."

"And you don't see a problem with that?" Her voice was very calm and quiet. I began to worry that this was a sign that an explosion was imminent. That this was merely a moment of calm before the storm.

"Um... no?" I said. "I mean, the way I see it, I'm helping people take advantage of the bank's multitude of services."

"Or you're helping the bank take advantage of regular people."

"Not at all! Look, this morning? I helped some guy get a second mortgage! He was so excited! He said he was finally going to start training monkeys to kickbox and make a documentary about it! He said that's always been his dream! I am helping him make that dream come true! And this other lady, she had no idea she was eligible for a five-thousand-dollar overdraft limit on her account! She wasn't sure she'd be able to buy groceries this week! Now she's taking her whole family out for steak dinners! See? I'm making the world a better place!"

Kalliope's face drained of all colour. "You've become a monster," she said. "You weren't like this before."

"Oh please," I said, running a hand through my hair. "You're just mad because I'm crazy successful now. You'll get over it. In fact, I'll help you get over it. Let's fly to Milan, first-class, and get couple of thousand-dollar meals. On me. You're welcome in advance."

Kalliope did something I never thought she was capable of. She pulled her right fist back and punched me in the face as hard as she could. Considering the strength it takes to fire arrows for hours on end every night, I shouldn't have been surprised that her punch sent me tumbling across the bank, colliding with the opposite wall. I slid down the wall, landing in a heap on the tile floor. Everything started fading. Kalliope flew over to me as my vision began to dim. Oh crap, I thought, is she coming to finish me off?

I was drifting away from consciousness. I felt something lift me off the ground. A moment later, I wasn't aware of anything at all.

***

Three weeks later, I was back at it. My nose was healing nicely. I was hovering about twenty feet away from a man and woman, arrow drawn back, waiting for the right moment to shoot. They were getting closer... almost... Not yet... Still not yet... Now!

I fired two shots in quick succession. Clean hits in both of their backs. They convulsed, and both began to point and speak. "Oh, look at that chipmunk! It's adorable!"

"That cardinal is just beautiful! What a gorgeous colour!"

"And the trees!"

"And the flowers!"

"The air is so fresh and clean!"

"I wish we could spend so much more time out here!"

"Yes! Let's leave our dreary office jobs and devote our lives to the environment!"

"Yeah! And let's go camping!"

They clasped hands and continued their stroll through the forest.

Yes, I'd changed careers yet again. After Kalliope decked me, she threatened to never speak to me again if I continued using my talents to scam people. So I quit sales and spent a couple of miserable weeks looking for cupid jobs online.

As an added bonus, I was back to being broke. If you think hospital bills are outrageous for humans, you should see the bill from a cupid hospital. Everything in the damn place has to be custom-made to be cupid-sized and must be crazy expensive to make. I don't know. Whatever the reason, getting my injuries from Kalliope's wrath tended to burned through most of my newfound wealth.

But I eventually found decent work. National parks were hiring cupids as part of a climate change initiative to help people fall in love with nature. I applied, got an interview, and got in. It's better than the love gig, that's for sure. I just fly around the parks, soaring over lakes, forests, and mountains, shooting anyone I find marvelling at the wilderness. The pay is okay. It's fine.

I watched the couple vanish into the forest and I sighed. For a few beautiful weeks, I was one of the richest and most successful cupids in the world. Now I work in a park. Still, it was way, way better than the love game.

Another couple came down the trail. My mind went blank and I took off, circling them a few times to get a sense of their movements and look for a clear shot. The woman froze and grabbed the man's arm. She pointed. There was an adorable little bunny on the edge of the path. I grinned and pulled two arrows from my quiver. Two nature-loving environmentalists, coming right up!

I Hate Instant Mashed Potatoes

I was smiling before I'd even turned my key in the lock of my apartment door. I could hear jazz playing inside. Jazz always meant something was up. Daniel must be planning something special. I wonder what it could be... maybe he finally got a better job somewhere. I stepped inside to find the lights dimmed, candles lit, and dinner waiting for me. My husband walked over to me with a glass of wine. "Happy anniversary," he said, kissing me on the cheek.

I accepted the wine and kissed him in return. "You remembered!" I said, taking a sip of the wine. Decent stuff. In truth, I'd totally forgotten today was our anniversary, but I was not about to show my hand. To my credit, I knew it was sometime in September, but even with a gun to my head, I'd be hard-pressed to get more specific than that. I'm hopeless with dates. "Come and sit down for dinner," Daniel said. "Let's eat while it's still hot!"

I joined him at the dinner table. It was elegant. Candles, the nice tableware my grandmother left me, and mountains of food. "I made all your favourites," Daniel said, putting our plates on the table. "Peppercorn steaks in a whiskey sauce, beet salad, grilled asparagus, and mashed potatoes."

The steak, salad, and asparagus looked flawless. Daniel was a bit on the dopey side, but a masterful cook. And the potatoes... oh, wait. Where were they? "Everything's perfect," I said. "But where are the mashed potatoes? No, don't get up, I can bring them out."

"I left them in the oven to keep them warm."

I opened the oven door and found the bowl they were in. The bowl was covered by a ceramic lid, and was perfectly warm to my touch. I set the bowl on the counter and took the lid off, determined to sneak a fingerful of mashed potatoes before I set them on the table. I set the lid down on the counter as stealthily as possible, and peered into the bowl.

Oh.

Oh God.

Please no.

I was too horrified to scream. I stood, frozen in sheer terror, staring at what lay in the bowl before me. It looked like drywall filler. Could it be what I thought it was? I prayed that it wasn't. I had to ask Daniel if he'd done what I feared he had. "So, you made mashed potatoes, sweetie?" I called, trying to sound casual.

"Well, instant mashed potatoes."

Fuck. My very worst fears had been confirmed. A numbness overcame me, leaving me unable to speak. Daniel continued. "I only had so much time to get everything ready! So I had to cut a corner and that was the easiest one. But they were on sale! And I made them with tons of butter and milk, so we probably won't notice the difference.

I doubted that.

My childhood revolved around this same prepackaged, inedible muck, and I hate it passionately. In the twenty years since then, it looked like instant mashed potatoes hadn't made the same progress as electric cars or smartphones. It was the same steaming slop I remembered as a child. It even smelled the same. Ugh. The contents of the bowl before me looked both chalky and gluey. I took a deep breath and brought the bowl to the table. Daniel peered at it. He must have thought they looked godforsaken too, because he said, "the colour is a little odd, but it smells lovely!"

I said nothing, determined not to spoil the mood. I was touched at what he'd done and didn't want to shut him down tonight. So I set the bowl of gloppy garbage on the table and vowed to ignore it. Daniel and I sat down for dinner and I helped myself to the dinner options that were genuinely delicious, and not simply pretending to be real food.

But the pretender-potatoes were as easy to ignore as a rotting corpse draped over our dinner table, and Daniel was too proud of his

31

efforts to let them die, however much they deserved to. "Here, have some potatoes, love," Daniel said, dropping a scoopful onto my plate with a watery splat.

If you think instant mashed potatoes look disgusting in a bowl, when they share a plate with real food, they look like an abomination that could not be of human creation. Nuzzled between Daniel's peppercorn steak and asparagus, it looked pathetic and undead. As the slop settled onto my plate, it seemed to be begging me to just eat it in a single mouthful and put it out of its miserable, godforsaken existence. To destroy it and never look back. I found myself hating it for existing, and considered avoiding it and everything they touched on my plate. I was just working up the courage to tell Daniel that I couldn't tolerate eating them, when he put a massive forkful of the sludge in his mouth and smiled. "Mm, yum," he said.

His smile vanished as he tried to chew the abominable substance and discovered its paradoxical texture that managed to be simultaneously dusty and moist. He gagged, valiantly fighting to chew, and managed to swallow the mouthful. "Delicious," he said, almost managing to sound sincere.

I love Daniel dearly, and I decided he couldn't go through this alone. We were partners in sickness and in health. He'd eaten my appalling cooking without complaint before he'd politely taken over all kitchen-related duties. I had to at least try the instant potatoes for him. Out of love for him, I took a moderate forkful, made peace with God, and put it in my mouth.

Oh. It's so— my god...

WHY?

The flakes that had been resistant to the milk and butter lacerated the inside of my mouth, while the gooey remainder tried to ooze out from between my lips. The gluey papier-mâché texture started wracking up paper-cuts on the insides of my cheeks and on my tongue. I tried to break down the concrete-like texture and consistency by chewing it, and that was a huge mistake. Letting it between my teeth simply made it easier for the substance to glue my jaw shut and froze me in mid-chew. Daniel was watching me like a dog waiting for a biscuit, hoping for approval for all of his efforts. I

I Hate Instant Mashed Potatoes

tried to smile, but I didn't dare move my lips for fear of throwing up. My mouth was frozen in place, and my eyes went wide with fear.

Daniel noticed.

"Sweetie, if it's crap, don't eat it," he said (to his credit).

"Nnnnnnnnm," I protested, fighting like a demon to chew or swallow the oozy, flechette-ridden sludge.

Okay, so I have to tell you something about myself that's quite personal: I have a gag reflex on a hair-trigger. I sometimes choke on my toothbrush, and putting anything big or gross in my mouth on a full stomach can lead to disaster. I'd already eaten most of my dinner, and I was trying to suppress my gag reflex as I choked on the potatoes, while I was also trying to wrench my mouth open. A disastrous combination. Because when I finally did manage to pry my jaws apart, I vomited all over the table, ruining everything.

***

Daniel was really good about it.

I came back from brushing my teeth and found him heating up a tin of soup on the stove. He hadn't eaten as quickly as I had, and I guess he was still hungry. I came up to him from behind and wrapped my arms around him. He didn't acknowledge me and seemed unusually focused on stirring his soup.

"I love you," I said.

"Yep."

Uncomfortable silence.

"Want to snuggle?"

"I'm making soup."

Further silence.

"After soup?"

"I... okay. Sure."

"And maybe we can listen to a podcast? While we snuggle?"

"Sounds good."

Daniel is a decent guy, he just needs to sulk for awhile after things go to shit. And given what happened, I thought a bit of sulking was justified. He tucked into his soup, and I went to the hall to put the tin in the recycling. The package for the instant mashed potatoes was in the bin, where it belonged. I picked it out of the recycling and read the back of the box:

33

MOLL'S INSTANT MASHED POTATOES

Need mashed potatoes in a hot minute? Moll's Instant Mashed Potatoes can be ready in five minutes and a single packet is enough to feed a whole family! Only the finest potatoes are selected for Moll's Instant mashed potatoes (what a tragedy, I lamented) *and our potatoes are augmented with jellyfish DNA to make them nice and squishy, wolverine DNA to make them hearty, and crocodile DNA to enhance their longevity! Enjoy the most resilient and long-lasting instant mashed potatoes from the cutting edge of modern science!*

Total bullshit, every word of it. I mean, I doubted they were anything more than subpar potatoes that wouldn't have made it to market otherwise. I threw the box back in the recycling and vowed to put them out of my mind. I went and checked on Daniel. He'd finished his soup, so I led him to bed, where I cuddled up against him. We put on a comedy podcast, and I started working on a plan to jump him, or at least give him a back rub to apologize for earlier. At least, that's what I was planning before I heard the sound of breaking glass coming from the kitchen. Daniel and I pulled apart and looked at each other. "Did I imagine that?" he asked.

"No, I heard it too. Should we go have a look?"

"Yeah."

We slipped from our bed and went to the hall. As soon as I stepped into the hall, I heard something tinkling in the kitchen. I hoped it was just the tap dripping, and that nothing weird was going on. And oh, how wrong I was.

You know how I said that instant mashed potatoes are an abomination? Well, I was right. Moreso than I ever could have imagined.

I stopped dead when I saw what was going on in the kitchen with the mashed potatoes. They had come to life, and from their behaviour, they were disposed towards violence and killing people.

I surmised this because the instant mashed potatoes had congealed into a humanoid being, perhaps two feet tall. It was gelatinous and stumpy, with bits of potato occasionally dripping off of it. The monster had crude mitts for hands, a gaping mouth for a face, and it was becoming even more nightmarish by the second.

You see, the monster had smashed the empty beer bottles Daniel and I kept under the sink, and it was embedding the shards in its mouth and mitts so it could have fangs and claws. Amber shards littered its jaw in rows, and longer shards stuck out from all over its mitts. It sat on the floor and picked through the shards for the most jagged ones, and jammed them in its mouth, one at a time. Suddenly, the monster stopped. It turned and looked at us, although it had no eyes to see with. Upon registering our presence, the massive mouth broke into a toothy grin and it stood up. The abomination opened and closed its jaws, bringing his jagged teeth down to meet with the scraping of glass. It then extended his claws and ran towards us.

Daniel screamed. I didn't even manage that, I just fled. Daniel followed and we retreated to the bedroom and locked the door. I pulled him back from it, and we waited, holding each other.

The overly-processed living nightmare stopped at the door. There was silence for a moment. Then came the first scrape.

Then the second.

Then the third, louder this time.

The abomination was trying to claw and bite through the door.

I turned to Daniel, "Call the police!"

"And tell them what, exactly?"

"Anything! Just get us help!"

Daniel stumbled to the bed to grab his phone. I just watched the door and listened to the scrapes against the wood. All of a sudden, it stopped. Daniel and I looked at each other. Was it giving up? Had it died? Were we safe?

I turned back and looked at the door. It wasn't budging, maybe the monster decided it couldn't cut through— but then I noticed something. There wasn't any light coming in from under the door anymore. Maybe the potato-demon was blocking it? Wait... what? Then I saw it, and I realized why no light was coming through.

It was coming in from under the door. Through the gap. Shit.

But it made sense. Whatever the hell was wrong with it, the monster was made of instant mashed potatoes. It didn't have to be solid. It could squeeze through cracks or gaps. There was no hiding

UNQUESTIONABLY MONSTROUS

from it. It was coming for us no matter what. Daniel must have realized this too, a little slow on the uptake, as usual, because he shrieked and pointed at the door. I scanned the room for a weapon. We didn't have much in the bedroom, really. Just our dresser, the bed, and a bookshelf.

On the dresser, though, was a can of hairspray. That might work, but only if...

I turned to Daniel, "Are you still smoking weed?"

"What? No! I told you I was giving it up!"

"Daniel! We don't have time for this! Just tell me: are you still smoking weed when I'm not around?"

"Why are you asking this now? Is this really the best time to work through stuff?"

"DANIEL!"

"Fine! Yes! Sometimes!"

"Where's your lighter?"

"Bedside table!"

I found it. The potato-demon was almost past the door, and was congealing back to its humanoid form only a few feet from Daniel and I. I grabbed the hairspray and prepared to strike. Would it die? Would it just keep charging? Could it even feel pain? I certainly hoped it could, and that this would stop it.

"Get ready," I said, holding up the hairspray and the lighter.

"Jesus Christ!" Daniel said. "You'll burn the building down!"

"Which is why you'll grab the fire extinguisher once you can get to the door! Go get it, run right back, and be ready to put the room out!"

Daniel nodded, eyes wide with fear. The potato-demon had made it into the room and was back to its humanoid form, claws and teeth barred. "GO!" I shouted at Daniel, taking aim.

Daniel tore the door open and ran, leaving me alone with the monster.

The lighter lit, I took aim with my hairspray flamethrower. The potato demon sensed an attack, and leapt from the jet of flames, on to my dresser. Without hesitation, the oozing monster leapt again, claws extended and jaws open to eviscerate me with its broken rows of glass teeth.

I don't know how I reacted so fast, but I ducked. The demon-taters missed me by inches, and landed on the bed with a splat. I pivoted, hairspray still raised and the lighter still lit, and shot a wave of fire at the wretched creature, catching it as it struggled to its feet. The abomination was engulfed in flame. It began to wither and let out a high-pitched scream. It stumbled and collapsed, still taking feeble swipes at me with its claws. Its claws raked the mattress, leaving deep gouges, but it advanced no further. The potato-demon let out a final gasp and collapsed, overcome by the flames.

The bedding was also catching fire, but Daniel came roaring in and aimed the fire extinguisher at the dead monster and the bedroom at large. He didn't stop until the canister was empty.

Can't fault him for enthusiasm.

As the chemical fog cleared, we were left standing in a powdery room, in front of a smouldering pile of instant mashed potatoes and glass. The bed was ruined, but we were unscathed.

The lighter and hairspray fell from my hands, and Daniel set down the fire extinguisher. We looked at each other as the fog settled.

"What do we do now?" Daniel asked.

"Want to sit on the balcony?"

"Wait, what? You want to just sit outside after all this?"

"Damn it, Daniel. Come on. We could use a quiet moment, we'll talk about it outside."

We went and sat out on the balcony, and held hands. After a while, Daniel said, "You know, I bought those from this weird little grocery store in the East End that sells experimental food. That could explain... everything. Those mashed potatoes must have been some kind of GMOs."

I didn't dignify that comment with an answer. I mean, they were clearly modified in some way, but I wasn't going to follow up on that one.

Daniel squeezed my hand and looked at me. "From now on, I'll make real mashed potatoes with dinner."

"Agreed."

Poetic Justice

"Oh fuck," Detective Rottmayer said.

He was standing in a murder victim's living room. The victim had been butchered well beyond being identifiable. Blood and viscera covered the walls. The smell was horrific. But that was nothing new to Detective Rottmayer, he'd seen all kinds of crazy shit and this wasn't the freakiest crime scene he'd ever come across.

No, what caused him to swear was a single page of paper pinned neatly to a far wall that had four lines of poetry typed on it. The lines read:

> *I never knew death had made incomplete*
> *So many. Lost, with fleeting joys and empty hearts.*
> *Men who dared not look beyond the cobblestones*
> *Who pour into the inhuman city down King William Street.*

Detective Rottmayer didn't know what those lines meant or where they came from. And this meant that Detective Rottmayer would have to work with an expert on poetry for this case. God damn it. Which meant partnering with the insufferable Detective Innis. Detective Innis was a cop with a Master's of English Literature. He was the force's 'literary specialist' and on those weird, fucked-up cases where the perpetrator left poetry or riddles or whatever pretentious bullshit at the crime scene, he'd identify and analyse it. And by God, did he make sure everyone knew why he was there when he was on a case.

Detective Rottmayer stood in the middle of the crime scene and savoured the silence before Innis arrived. And good thing he did, because the son of a bitch burst onto the crime scene barely a minute later, gasping and panting.

"Rottmayer! Hi! The chief called me in! I caught a ride with the coroner! Another poetry murder? Excellent! I mean, what a horrible tragedy. But thank God I'm here! Hopefully, I'll be able to find the implicit meaning of the poetry and we'll catch this fiend in his tracks!"

Rottmayer gave the first of what was sure to be many, many sighs. "What makes you think this is the work of a man?"

Innis gave a loud, cawing laugh. "My good man! Poetry is an inherently masculine art! All the great epics are written in verse! Renaissance poetry is rife with powerful men describing their romantic conquests. Poetry is the muscle on the skeleton of the written word! Our killer is obviously an intelligent and ferocious alpha-male," Innis said. "Also, he's probably incredibly dangerous. And violent. Probably good-looking. Absolutely jacked."

Rottmayer had also gathered that whoever had done this was ferocious, dangerous, and violent from a first glance at the eviscerated corpse. But sure. This guy was *the* poetry expert. Maybe he knows what he's talking about. Maybe.

Innis was, at least, kitted out in proper crime scene gear. He was in a protective bodysuit with a mask and goggles. His long brown hair and scraggly goatee were hidden, but he was still identifiable by his lean frame and arrogant gait. Innis clasped his hands behind his back and sauntered over to the page that was pinned on the wall, and read the verse printed upon it. "Ah-ha!" he said.

"Do you know what it means?" Rottmayer asked.

"Hmm? No. That was only a preliminary reading. Meaning will come later. Subtextual interpretation will come after that. But I recognize it. This is from S.T. Emmerson's *The Ruined World*."[1]

---

[1] Saunders Taylor Emmerson (September 27th, 1888 – January 5th, 1965) was a poet, playwright, and literary critic. Considered one of the foremost poets of the 20th century, he is a key figure in the Modernist movement. He earned widespread acclaim for his poem *The Ruined World* in 1922. His children's book, *Old Hatters Book of Wonderful Weasels*, was the basis for the 1981 stage musical, *Weasels*. A film adaptation of the musical was released in 2019 to vitriolic reviews and the film's production company is currently for sale. His works are *still* under copyright in the United Kingdom and Europe under Fibber Publishing.

"And that's all you have so far?"

"My dear man! These words are not some mere grocery list you can simply scan and understand! The crusade that is understanding poetry requires countless readings. Generations of scholars and brilliant minds deciphering and arguing over every word for decades or even centuries! But, I have the skills to compress decades of thought into mere minutes! Be silent a moment and let me think!"

Rottmayer obliged. Innis slouched over the printed page for a few minutes and there was silence. Rottmayer savoured the silence. All too soon, Innis turned back to Rottmayer and said, "I've got it."

Innis sat down in a chair that was untouched by the carnage. "Okay. Our killer is a man. He is obsessed with death. He is socially awkward and a societal outcast."

That sounded plausible, so far. Rottmayer gazed at Innis with newfound respect. Maybe he's actually got some serious skills in that brain of his—

"But our killer's main fixation, his obsession, is sex."

Uh-oh.

"Yes," Innis said, misreading Rottmayer's stunned silence as impressed or perhaps approving. His look of exasperation was hidden by his mask, goggles, and hairnet. "The line '*Lost, with feeling joys and empty hearts*' is clearly a reference to sexual intercourse. Casual gay sex, specifically."

Uh...

"And the second line backs this up further. With '*Men who dared not look beyond the cobblestones*' the killer is clearly alluding to his repressed gay desires he can only express in anonymous settings like the YMCA and gay bathhouses. Through anonymous hookup websites and apps."

"Gay guys hook up at the YMCA fitness centre? That's hilarious."

"And the final line is pure wish fulfilment. Our killer wishes in his heart of hearts that all the men who live in his city were also ferocious, fearless, and promiscuous gay men so that he could enact his wildest fantasies with them, unendingly and eternally! So that he could finally revel in his desires and say, 'See, mom? It's not a phase I'm going through and I love who I am and I'm happy for myself and all the wonderful experiences I'll have with the incredible people I'll meet!

So take that and stop trying to set me up with girls! I'm gay and you just have to deal with it!'"

Innis' voice had risen throughout his *purely* textual analysis and had evaporated to a shriek by the time he'd finished talking. He sat in his chair, taking shallow, panicked breaths. After a moment, he regained his composure. "That," he added, "is the mind I discover when I reach into these words for deeper meaning. A totally detached, purely academic analysis. So there you have it. What's our next move?"

"That's the whole point of the poem? The killer is telling us he is really, really gay and way the hell back in the closet? Who cares? Why bother telling us that?"

Innis gave another of his cawing laughs, this one louder than the last. "You homicide cops are all the same! Did you expect this to be some kind of riddle or anagram that would just tell us his identity or address? No, think! Really think for a minute! These scant lines of verse hold so much more than that! We have a motive! We have a drive! We know this man's purpose on Earth! I can see into his very mind! I can predict his next move!"

"Great," Rottmayer said. "So what's he going to do next?"

"What I meant," Innis added hastily, "is that I will soon be able to predict his next move."

"How soon? He could be making his next move now."

"Ah-ha!"

"What?"

"My theory is compelling! You clearly think our perpetrator is male! You weren't so sure before my close reading!"

Rottmayer's cell phone rang. He stepped into the hall to answer it. While he was out, Innis reread the poem, growing more confident by the moment that his reading was infallible. A moment later, Rottmayer returned. Innis couldn't make out his expression through his protective gear, but his posture suggested defeat and shock. "What is it?" Innis asked.

"There's been another murder. At 1965 King Street. Same M.O. as this one."

***

The car ride to the next crime scene was plagued with an uncomfortable silence. So Rottmayer dared to ask a personal question. "So. You working on a book?"

"Of course I am."

"What's it about?"

Innis sighed. "A great work of literature cannot be simply summed up as *about* something. It is a tapestry of life. Of victories and failures. Of hopes and battles of both the mind and body. I could no more tell you what my book is 'about' than tell you what the Universe or the oceans are 'about'."

"But it has a plot, right?"

"Oh yes. It is a coming-of-age story about a lost and brilliant young writer in university who has to discover where he wants to go in life and what kind of man he wants to become. It's sure to be a ground-breaking novel."

"Ground-breaking? You mean no one has written a novel like that before?"

"There have been feeble attempts."

"Alright then."

They continued in silence. Rottmayer was mulling over the poem from the last murder scene. *Men who dared not look beyond the cobblestones/Who pour into the inhuman city down King William Street.* The last line with an 'inhuman city' struck him as a strange idea. Cities were the most human places in the world. Humans built them. What is inhuman about them? Hell, King William Street is probably as normal as any other city in...

Wait a minute. He had it.

"Do you have a smartphone?" He asked Innis.

"Yes. Why?"

"Open your maps app. Look up 1965 King Street. What's near it?"

Innis poked at his phone screen and squinted at it. "Well, it looks like 1965 King Street is right at the corner of King Street and William Street—"

"Son of a bitch!"

"What?"

"He told us the location of the next murder! In the poem! He gave himself away!"

Innis looked up from his phone, brow furrowed. "Oh. I suppose he did."

"How did you miss that?"

"I," replied a haughty Detective Innis, "was looking deeper than the mere words on the page, my good man! For that is studying Literature."

"No! I don't know what you were doing, but it had nothing to do with the poem! You were just using the poem to work out some stuff you've got going on!"

"What? How dare you! Pull this car over this instant!"

"No! We have a murder scene to get to!"

Innis fumed and looked away. Rottmayer felt he'd overstepped, and decided to do some damage control. "Look," he said. "Maybe you were actually reading into something in the poem that's beneath the surface. Fine. But if not, if that was something you just projected onto it... just know that being gay or being different, or not fitting in somehow, that's fine. Whatever is eating at you. It's probably not a big deal. Just be you. The hell with people who can't handle it. Okay?"

Innis didn't answer right away. He continued staring out the window while shabby little houses and gruff, miserable people passed by. "Just... drive," he finally said.

***

The second murder scene was much like the first. The victim hadn't been as viciously brutalized, and was easy enough to identify as the tenant of the worn and crumbling bungalow he'd been murdered in. A middle-aged man who managed a shoe store. No enemies. No debts. Even so, the murder scene was gory and there was another piece of poetry pinned to the far wall:

> *The roar of motors and horns, which announce*
> *Mrs. Russell is to away for the summer.*
> *O the stars cast their cold light on Mrs. Russell*
> *And upon her only daughter.*

Innis seemed determined to outdo his previous work and read the poem over several times before he ventured to comment. Once he was prepared, he turned to Rottmayer and said, "I was mistaken."

"Oh?"

"Yes. Our killer isn't a closet homosexual. Our killer is fixated on incestuous fantasies."

"What?!"

"I know. It is a startling revelation. That... um... queer theory... from before? Yes, disregard that. I see now that I was looking at a single piece of the puzzle."

"So... our killer isn't gay? But he or she has a thing for a family member?"

"Precisely!" Encouraged, Innis began to pace. "Yes... I see it so clearly now. *The Ruined City* is a 20th century poem. To solve the mystery of the killer's identity, we need to use 20th century literary theory. Specifically, the theoretical work of Sigmund Freud.[2] Yes... every detail and lost strand is falling into place. The poetry from the first crime scene refers to men who have been symbolically castrated by their fathers as punishment for having incestuous thoughts about their mothers."

"Sorry?!"

"Meanwhile, women, who have no fear of castration, can entertain fantasies of incest without repercussion! The description of Mrs. Russell and her daughter under the moonlight is clearly an erotic dream of incest, and our killer is expressing their warped desires through murder! Which makes perfect sense because death is always historically connected to the org—"

"I'm sorry, but you learned this when you were studying English lit? Like, a professor or someone actually said all of this to you, in a classroom, with a straight face? About symbolic castration and incest and all this weird shit?"

---

[2] Unlike S. T. Emmerson, Freud's writings *are* in the Public Domain.

"It's not weird shit! It's literary theory and it is the highest calling of the human mind!"

"For fuck's sake!" Rottmayer couldn't contain his temper a moment longer. "You are making this way more complicated than it needs to be! This is not some queer theory exercise! Or a meditation on the nature of incest, Dr. Freud! Someone, we don't know who, is on a murder spree and the son of a bitch is laying it out for us! The first poem gave us the location of the second murder! The second poem is probably giving us the name of the third victim! Take your head out of your godforsaken, reeking ass and just read the damn lines!"

Innis had taken a few steps back at Rottmayer's outburst. Although he was cowering at Rottmayer's wrath, he was still defiant. "Fine! Let's say you're right! Let's say that you, a homicide detective with the barest semblance of an intellect, a reader of James Patterson novels, if you read fiction at all, is correct. That a Mrs. Russell is his next victim. What do we even do with that? We don't have a full name; there could be a dozen women with that last name in the city!"

"He referenced Mrs. Russell and her daughter! There must be some way to find them! Can we find them on Facebook or LinkedIn or something?"

Innis pulled out his phone and did the one thing that all English majors unquestionably know how to do. He entered his passcode and googled the part of the poem that he was stuck on. A deft and underappreciated skill that had made thousands of English majors seem cleverer and more informed than they actually were. A simple trick that has allowed untold legions to seem competent and capable of critical thinking. And, as it always has and always will, it worked.

"Russell and Daughters," Innis said, not looking up from his phone. "It's a restaurant on Westborough. 20 minutes from here."

"Jesus Christ! Let's go!"

***

The restaurant windows were dark. It had closed hours ago.

Rottmayer hammered on the door hard enough to shake the adjacent windows. "Police!" he shouted. "Open this door immediately or I'm kicking it down!"

Silence. Rottmayer and Innis stood on the doorstep, waiting. Then, the sound of shattering glass. That was enough justification for Rottmayer to kick in the door and let Detective Innis and himself inside the restaurant. Guns drawn, they entered the dining area. Nothing. No signs of a struggle or forced entry. "Let's go upstairs," Rottmayer said. "Watch my back."

There was a small apartment upstairs where the restaurant owner, Mrs. Russell, lived with her daughter. Rottmayer steeled himself as he crossed the living room and went to the first bedroom door. He opened it. Nothing. He walked to the second bedroom door. He was nervous this time. He might find them, dead or dying in pools of arterial blood. He might come face-to-face with the killer. He took a deep breath, and opened the door.

The would-be killer was gone. Mrs. Russell was cowering in a corner, clutching her sobbing daughter. The bedroom window had been shattered. Rottmayer knelt down in front of Mrs. Russell, holstering his gun. "Ma'am, I'm with the police. Are you alright? Have either of you been harmed?"

"Oh my god! He said he was going to kill us! He told us to lay down on the floor! But before he did anything else, he walked over to the wall and pinned a piece of paper to it! It's still there!"

So it was. Rottmayer nodded, still kneeling on the floor. While Rottmayer tried to calm the Russells, Innis walked over to it and read the poem:

> *O inhuman city, of unending noise.*
> *Above a tawdry bar on Richmond Street*
> *I hear the pleasant purring of a guitar*
> *And voices and vices from within.*

Sirens. Backup was coming. Innis had called it in on the way over. The inbound officers could look after the Russells. Rottmayer and Innis were hot on the trail and had to stay on the killer. Innis finished re-reading the poem and turned to Rottmayer. "Any theories?" Rottmayer asked, malice in his voice. "Are we looking for a gay flirt, or an incest-obsessed young woman? Or maybe the guitar is the key to this one and we're looking for someone who has a fetish for professional musicians?"

"No," Innis said, scowling. "He means the Hare and the Fiddle. It's a bar on Richmond Street that has live music. It's also a cheap and scuzzy hotel. That's where we'll find him. He'll be waiting for us."

Rottmayer nodded at Innis. All his pomp and swagger was gone. He'd been chastised and humbled and was now a furious, sharp instrument. And he'd solved a clue that Rottmayer never would have gotten. An alcoholic, now fifteen years sober, Rottmayer only set foot in bars if they were murder scenes. Or to apprehend suspects. Rottmayer just hoped that whatever they found above the bar hotel wasn't as gruesome as the lifetime of nightmares they'd seen so far.

***

The Hare and the Fiddle is putrid in every respect. From the sickly yellow colour of the exterior bricks to the smoke-stained, grimy barroom walls and blackened wooden floors. The tables and bar are scored with scorch marks from the cigarettes and pipes of long-dead smokers. It is where you go to drink if you've been forbidden from drinking anywhere else. There's a hotel above the bar where bedbugs thrive and you can come and go with no questions asked. This was where the trail had led. Rottmayer started for the tavern door, and noticed Innis hanging back. "You okay?"

Innis nodded and gulped. "Anything could be waiting for us in there."

Rottmayer nodded. "And that's why there's two of us. We'll look out for each other."

Innis didn't look entirely reassured, but he gave another nod and followed Rottmayer up to the bar. Rottmayer approached the wrinkled and bearded bartender. Rottmayer didn't bother making small talk. "Detective Innis and I are looking for someone who's been staying here. Someone who likes poetry and shit. You see anyone like that?"

"Oh Jesus," the barkeep said, hands in the air as if the detectives had their guns drawn. "No. I mean, yeah. The guy in 316. He seems to be reading all the time when he's drinking. Old poetry and stuff. He just came in. He's all yours."

"Stay where you are. Advise anyone you see to go to their rooms and stay there."

"Holy shit. Yes sir!"

Rottmayer and Innis started up the stairs to the hotel. The wooden steps didn't creak so much as they shrieked in protest with each step. If the killer was waiting for them, it was a good bet he knew they were there. But there was nothing else for it at this point. They had to press on.

Rottmayer and Innis stopped outside room 316 and drew their guns.

Rottmayer was in no mood to knock. Innis stood back, gun drawn, and Rottmayer gave the wooden door to the room a kick, ripping apart the crumbling lock and blasting the door open. Guns drawn, Innis and Rottmayer peered into the room. "Police! Don't move!"

The man in the room obliged. He did not move a muscle. He was sitting at a battered wooden writing desk with his back to the detectives. Rottmayer could see he was small and slender man, but could not yet see his face. Rottmayer and Innis approached their suspect, guns drawn, and Rottmayer got a look at the suspect's face. He was man in his fifties with wild, unkempt hair and a pair of wire spectacles that magnified his eyes, with the overall effect of making him look like an owl that had just been electrocuted.

Rottmayer and Innis stood on either side of him, guns unwavering. The man decided it was safe to move, and he set down his pen and smiled at the detectives. "My," he said. "That was quick. Please come in."

"You were expecting us?" Rottmayer asked.

"Of course," the killer said. "The clues were meant to lead you to me eventually. But I am rather impressed with how quickly you put the clues together."

An increasingly smug Detective Innis let out his trademark cawing laugh. "Why, I more than solved where your hideout was! I learned to effortlessly navigate the labyrinth of your mind!"

"Did you, now?" The killer gave Innis an encouraging smile. "And what is my motive, pray tell?"

Innis started to answer, but Rottmayer cut him off. "No, stop it. This is no time for games," I turned back to the killer. "Why'd you do it?"

The man looked out the grimy window and sighed. "It was my way of saying goodbye to Dorothy."

"Dorothy?"

"My wife. She's dying. Cancer, if you'd like to know."

"And you're, what, getting back at her enemies?" Rottmayer asked. "You're settling her scores?"

"Oh, nothing so fancy," the killer said. "She loves poetry. She loves theatre. And she was fuckin' obsessed with true crime podcasts."

Innis and Rottmayer waited for the killer to elaborate, but that seemed to be all. "Sorry," Rottmayer said. "You went on a poetry-themed, murderous rampage because your dead wife was into true crime?"

"Well, there'll be a podcast on the murders before too long. Probably several. They're desperate for content. And Dorothy would have listened to my exploits with joy in her heart. She listened to true crime podcasts until it made her afraid to leave the house! I wanted to give her one last favourite true-crime podcast."

Rottmayer found this motive far more disturbing than if the killer had been settling scores. This sick fuck was just killing random people to get famous. The worst kind of murder. The devilish work of a monster. A man seeking glory. Innis, however, was reinvigorated by this info and seemed on the verge of doing a jig.

Yes, with the murderer cornered and Innis responsible for the clue that led right to him, Innis regained his lost pomp and swagger, and was back to being a certified literary expert and detective. "Oh ho! I was right," he cried. "I was right the whole time! The killer was primarily motivated by a repressed sexual desire! But not gay sex! Minor misread, I admit. But the sex he can no longer have with his wife! A wife who he considered family! Through the bonds of marriage! So the motive was totally a repressed sexual longing for a lost family member! My analysis was flawless!"

"Is that true?" Rottmayer asked the killer, baiting Innis. "Was that what you were trying to tell us with your poetry clues?"

"What the hell? No. The little dude is seriously overthinking this," the killer said. "I just picked that S. T. Emmerson poem because it's so goddamn long and specific, I figured it would be easy to make clues out of. There's no magic to any of it."

Innis' face went red with rage. "Bullshit! My theory is brilliant! It's flawless! I can back it up with quotes! It has to be true! If only on a subconscious level! If it can be found, it is there! Even if the author never intended it or vehemently disagrees!"

"That sounds like a licence to put words in peoples' mouths," the killer said.

"Yeah," Rottmayer said to Innis. "You're really overthinking this."

Innis, inches from a full-blown-tantrum, stomped his foot. "No! No! I am not arresting our suspect until someone acknowledges my brilliance! Someone has to tell me my theory makes sense and is really smart, because otherwise, otherwise..."

Innis, spitting with rage and twitching like a drowning bug, clutched at his gun as if he were going to snap it in half. "Because otherwise I have a useless degree in English literature and I'm not really a specialized detective! I'm just a fool who paid tens of thousands of dollars to read books! I could have done that for free! So somebody, anybody, tell me I solved the case and that I'm brilliant or, so help me God, I will snap!"

Part of Rottmayer wanted to see Innis snap. For a moment, he strongly considered doing nothing and watching the meltdown of the century. But, the gentler side of him had to acknowledge Innis had solved the final clue that led to the suspect. And, if you omitted or ignored all the details of Innis's theory, it had been kind-of accurate.

"Your theory is brilliant," Rottmayer said. "And you're the reason we found our suspect. We couldn't have done it without an English major."

Innis instantly calmed down. His composure regained, he pulled out a pair of handcuffs. He read the killer his rights and cuffed him. As they led the killers down the stairs, a question sprang to Rottmayer's mind. "Are you an English major as well?" he asked the killer.

"Communications, actually. So the skills from English lit but with the promise of a career afterwards."

"Ah-ha!" Innis cried. "Again, thank goodness I was here! It takes an English major to outwit a communications major!"

Rottmayer and the killer shared an exasperated look and Rottmayer led on. Detective Innis followed, humming to himself, wondering how best to phrase his request for a raise and a promotion to the Chief of Police the next time he saw him.

Latheck: The Climate Change Barbarian

Fenisys was cowering under a dry, dead shrub. He was a scholar, not a man of the forest, and was terrified of the monsters and beasts that were rumoured to dwell within the great Ashea forest of Zevren. Swamp creatures. Man-eating beasts with yellow eyes, rumoured to soundlessly hunt lost travellers in perfect darkness. The very thought made him anxious and sweaty. He suspected he would throw up before the day's light had died. Extreme nervousness and stress always made Fenisys physically sick. And if any nearby monster heard the retching, it would find him and eat him alive. The realization increased his terror, and he became certain he would throw up any moment now.

But something made him forget his terror. A voice. "Fenisys? Damnit boy, where are you? Come out from wherever you are hiding. We have urgent work before us!"

Fenisys crawled out from his shrub, "Latheck? Is that you?"

"Oh, there you are. Why were you hiding in a bush?"

Shame washed over Fenisys as he searched for the words to explain how terrified he was of his surroundings. He decided to lie. "I thought I saw a rare insect, O great barbarian of social justice. I wanted to observe it in its natural habitat."

Fenisys approached Latheck, his hero and mentor. The barbarian of a thousand legends. The hero who had conquered the Kingdom of Zevren without so much as drawing his blade. He was tall and muscular, with long black hair, thick-rimmed glasses, a "LOVE TRUMPS HATE" tattoo, and several facial piercings. Latheck scowled when he heard his former title. "I am no longer a barbarian of social justice. Where in the ten hells have you been? I am now Latheck the Climate Change Barbarian. And today, you and I shall stop the great climate change of Zevren in its tracks!"

Indeed, our hero had taken on a new calling! Climate change! And Fenisys had been assigned to Latheck as a graduate student apprentice. Their noble work was moments away from changing the world. Latheck, the barbarian formerly known for social justice, had ascended to the throne of Zevren and had transformed the crumbling empire into a progressive utopia! The same instant the crown touched his head, he decreed that everyone could be referred to by whatever pronouns they wished. He allowed people of any background, race, or sexuality to marry whomever they desired. He enacted equal salaries for men and women. Abortions for anybody who wants one! All bathrooms in the empire became gender-neutral! And the people worshipped him!

However, Latheck soon realized governing the Zevren Empire also meant making difficult and unpopular decisions. He would have to decide if the Empire continued its war/occupation/nation-building experiment on the distant island of Seaguard. Not a problem with a simple answer. His elderly advisors were clueless and led him to make unwise decisions. The vitriol of his political enemies demoralized him. So Latheck called for an early election, propped up a straw-man opponent to replace him, and lost power. But it was not truly a defeat! It was the freeing of an untamed and rugged barbarian! Latheck now knew that he was no shiftless politician, languishing on a throne! He was a barbarian of action! Within an hour of the election results, Latheck had traded in his court finery for his trusty wooden armour, and returned to wandering the wilds of the Zevren Empire, and had sought out a new crusade.

"Social justice is an old quandary," Latheck said. "And one that I single-handedly solved! For I was once a cast-aside member of a downtrodden minority because I am a polyamorous, sapiosexual, 1/64th Indigenous, vegan atheist. But I have since realized that I am a victim of so, so much more! Climate change! So now I am a polyamorous, sapiosexual, 1/64th Indigenous, vegan, atheist environmentalist! Because the unseen, nigh-unvanquishable foe that is climate change is set to leave no corner of the globe untouched! And it is already making food scarce! And parts of the empire unlivable! Let's see my critics call me a 'whiny pain-in-the-ass' now! Because, my brother, now I am whining about an actual, urgent crisis and people can't just tell me to shut up and go away!"

Latheck grinned. Fenisys was inspired by Latheck's unvanquishable spirit. Latheck clapped a hand on his young apprentice's shoulder. "Come!" Latheck said. "We have a climate to save! Did you bring the supplies I requested?"

"Yes sir!" Fenisys opened his pack and gave the barbarian the items he'd requested. A piece of flint and a chunk of fool's gold. "But, O great barbarian, how shall we stop this monstrous climate change with these pieces of rock?"

"By doing a great service to the environment. We will be doing a controlled burn of this ancient, dry forest to ensure it cannot be the heart of a devastating forest fire."

A controlled burn (when executed by professionals with permits under strict regulations) is when a fire is intentionally set to burn off dead and dry brush in a forest, to ensure it cannot be fuel for a severe and devastating fire in the hot season. The Indigenous peoples of Zevren had been doing them for thousands of years before the pale race arrived. The pale race, however, decided controlled burns would a) be expensive b) get in the way of the forestry industry, so the practice was outlawed. For it is difficult to clear-cut forests amidst carefully-maintained, regularly-occurring fires. Besides, unmanaged forests looked more regal in tourism advertisements. So the government abdicated management of the forests entirely and assumed they would stand forever.

Except that as the climate grew hotter, the forests grew drier and burned down in horrific fires anyway. Desperate to preserve the sprawling and lucrative Noveer forest to the south, and the picturesque tourist-friendly Ashea forest to the north, the government contracted a slew of private fireguards to maintain them. Latheck, finding that his slam-poetry readings and self-published tirades on his oppression were not keeping him fed and sheltered, had applied to manage the Ashea forest in the north, which had been devastated by an unrelenting drought.

Anyway, planning and nuance did not trouble the warlike mind of Latheck, who walked over the dry brush Fenisys had been hiding under, flint and rock in hand. "Come, my apprentice! We shall burn this dry brush with the utmost caution to ensure it cannot become the catalyst for a raging wildfire. So that these trees shall instead be renewed, to store carbon and have a cooling effect on the empire! Until the lumber industry comes for them. Aid me, my brother, in this noble work!"

Fenisys watched as Latheck struck the flint against the fool's gold, creating a shower of sparks with every hit. After several strikes, the sparks caught the dry brush, and the first flames began to creep along the dead branches, engulfing the rest of the shrub. It was ablaze in mere moments. Latheck and Fenisys retreated as the fire spread to other dry shrubs and trees. Latheck grinned with satisfaction, and Fenisys watched the blaze in awe. As the fire grew in strength by the second, Fenisys turned to Latheck. "And how shall we slow the blaze, O great barbarian? How shall we control this mighty fire?"

Latheck cocked an eyebrow. "You are the apprentice sent to me from the University of Zevren. You will be the one to cast spells and control the fire. That is what you have been taught, yes? I am merely the spark. You shall guide it and prevent it from destroying the empire."

Fenisys froze. This information had not been relayed to him previously. He had brought a flask of water and a small pail to pour sand on a campfire, but did not have the means to halt the growing inferno. "Sirrah! I can no more stop the blaze than I can stop the spinning of the Earth or the ebb and flow of the tides! The world's climate is too vast for any single sorcerer to control!"

Latheck's smirk changed to a look of terror in an instant. "What in the ten hells? Are you serious, boy?"

"Yes! This fire shall consume this forest and all that dwells within it!"

"Then what good is an intern from the University of Zevren's climate change program? What in the ten hells are they teaching you, if not spells to magically fix our climate?"

"Carbon accounting, mostly! How to make Zevren a net-zero empire! Yesterday I had a class on the slowdown of the ocean's currents due to the melting of the Ice Kingdom!"

"By Jakartaria's fury! Run!"

Latheck turned on his heel and sprinted from the growing fire as fast as his wooden armour would allow. Fenisys dropped his supplies and ran after the great barbarian. The air grew thick with smoke, clawing at Fenisys's lungs as he ran. The smoke grew such that Fenisys could barely make out the barbarian running ahead of him, but he ran on. Just as Fenisys feared that exhaustion would overtake him, he and Latheck reached the edge of the forest, which gave way to a rolling valley and distant, snow-capped mountains. Fenisys doubled over, hands on his knees, gasping for air. Meanwhile, Latheck's former crusade for social justice had left him used to sprinting from danger and differing opinions, and he simply put his hands on his hips and grinned. "We did it, young apprentice! We are one step closer to solving climate change!"

Fenisys was too winded to speak, but managed to give Latheck a quizzical look.

"Think, young apprentice! Think! All the forest creatures who die in this blaze will no longer breathe! Which means they can no longer emit carbon dioxide! That is a weighty reduction of the empire's emissions. Plus, everything that is currently on fire was already at risk of catching fire! We aid this world by accelerating the renewal process! Because of us, a newer, greener forest can grow where this decrepit one stood! That new forest will absorb many greenhouse gas emissions!" Latheck began to pace. "Plus, the empire has a serious hovel shortage. Some of that forest will now be cleared, and upon it, affordable hovels can be built. Net-zero hovels that will be built to new building codes and have very low emissions. Which is what the empire needs to save our climate! Not silly forests, full of thieves and bandits and killers."

Fenisys was dizzy from smoke and delirious from the trauma of escaping the fire. In this mindset, he had to admit Latheck's logic made a certain amount of sense. He smiled and stood up. "It sounds to me like we are one step closer to solving the great calamity of climate change, O mighty barbarian!"

"Indeed, we are!" Latheck cried. "This is easy!"

What was not so easy was deciding where to go next. While Latheck was confident that he and Fenisys would be welcomed back to the capital city as heroes, the raging forest fire made it impossible to return there. Latheck was trying to remember if there were any university towns nearby where they could find some food and ale, perhaps listen to some slam poetry, when Fenisys pointed towards the mountains. "What is that over there?"

"What are you pointing at, young apprentice?"

"It looks like there is a walled city, at the base of those mountains!"

Latheck squinted. There was a settlement in the distance. But he could not make out any details. "Let us have a look," Latheck said. "We need somewhere to rest until the fire subsides. Perhaps they will feed and shelter us for the night."

Latheck and Fenisys made their way across the valley to the city. It was a long journey. The sun was setting by the time they arrived. The city was made of gleaming white stone, and Fenisys thought it looked to be circular. No towers ascended above the mighty walls. They followed a stone road to two gigantic brass doors. They were closed, but not barred. They had not seen a soul during their journey. Fenisys was starting to worry that whatever was ahead could be dangerous. He felt like he was going to throw up again. "This mighty city is deserted. Perhaps we would be better to turn around."

"We have nothing to lose by knocking on the door," Latheck said, without slowing his pace. "And they have no choice but to let me in and be respectful towards me! For I am a polyamorous, sapiosexual, 1/64th Indigenous, vegan, atheist, environmentalist, and the former ruler of Zevren! To refuse me entry would be bigoted, intolerant, transphobic, racist, and treason! If any reside within those walls, they will be forced to accommodate us for fear of being discriminatory! Or I shall cancel them with my trusty axe."

This reassured Fenisys, who was glad to be travelling with so capable and diverse a companion. Latheck approached the doors and knocked.

They waited in silence. Latheck knocked again. Nothing. The lack of response triggered Latheck, who drew his axe in a frenzy of bloodlust. "This is clearly an act of micro-aggression!" he roared.

"You, the people behind these doors, are infringing upon my rights! Equality and fairness mean I get to do whatever I want whenever I want! Therefore, let me into your home!"

"The doors may be unlocked," Fenisys said, "shall we try to open them?"

Latheck let out a roar and pushed against one of the doors with all his might. The door pushed open, revealing a long, stone hallway. "Oh," Latheck said, returning his axe to his belt. "Never mind. I am not being oppressed."

Latheck and Fenisys walked down the stone hallway, which was lit by lanterns filled with glowing stones. The stones gave off an unearthly blue light, but allowed them to proceed without fear of ambush. After a minute of walking, Latheck and Fenisys stepped into the center of the town.

It was perfectly round, and the only part of the city open to the smoky sky. A fountain sloshed away in the center. The fountain's statues showed two men and two women. They were powerful and beautiful, and all four were clasping hands, looks of trust and determination on their faces. The fountain was surrounded by benches and pathways, with empty flowerbeds where sprawling gardens once stood. Several shops faced the square, long since boarded up and abandoned. Ahead of the adventurers, the center split into two paths. One went to the left, and the other to the right.

"Could there be any survivors, O great barbarian? Or looters? Or monsters?"

"I know not. We should split up and search the pathways. Look for food, a comfortable place to sleep, or any inhabitants. We can meet back here in an hour."

Fenisys flinched. "Is that wise? What if there is an ambush?"

"Yell if you encounter danger," Latheck said. "I will come running. I shall go to the left, and you shall go to the right. Be careful, young apprentice. We shall see each other soon."

With that, Latheck took off down the left passage, leaving Fenisys standing alone. Fenisys swallowed and clenched his teeth. He set down the path on the right, into the depths of the city.

***

Latheck wandered the halls of the empty city, finding nothing he was searching for. The halls were lit by the eerie blue rocks whose light never waned. But there was no sign of any inhabitants. He searched deep within the left, delving into its core. He wandered up and down stairways, and was close to giving up when he turned a corner and found himself held at spearpoint. A young woman was holding the spear and she looked as astonished to see Latheck as he was to see her. "Who are you?" she asked. "And what are you doing in the left side of Dividika?"

"My name is Latheck the barbarian. And I am a polyamorous, sapiosexual, 1/64th Indigenous, vegan, atheist, environmentalist, and the former ruler of Zevren! Who are you?"

The woman lowered her spear and gave Latheck a once-over. If she found him bizarre, she did not show it. "My name is Ziathian," she said. "And I am one of the guards of the left. Behind this door is the last stronghold of my people. We are in perilous times, great barbarian. Tell me, have you any food? Any provisions?"

"None," Latheck said. "I was hoping you could provide me with some."

"Oh, woe!" Ziathian cried. "For we are starving! We have not food to survive the winter!"

"What has happened?" Latheck asked. "Have your crops failed?"

"No, they flourish!" Ziathian wailed. "But last year they were genetically modified to withstand droughts and my tribe refuses to eat them! They consider modified food an unnatural blight on this Earth! Most will only eat organic produce, and there is not enough of it to sustain us all!"

"And you will not even feed the modified crops to hungry children?" Latheck asked. "Surely inorganic food is better than starving, even if inorganic food is a lesser, tasteless mockery of real food!"

"Ha! There is no danger of that. For no child has been born to our tribe in the last ten years," Ziathian said, her expression turning prideful. "We are too progressive to procreate. For the act of a man impregnating a woman was deemed patriarchal, as no egg can truly consent to being colonized by an invasive sperm that will determine the egg's sex and gender at birth, likely against its will. Thus, all procreation stopped in the name of equality."

"So you are at risk of extinction, then?"

"I... yes. I suppose so. But the patriarchal act of fornication dies with us!"

Latheck approved. "As it shall be! May you practice pegging and dry-humping with the knowledge that you have defeated an ancient heteronormative doctrine! But I must ask, can you spare me any inorganic food? My companion and I need rest and shelter."

"Yes, you can take as much inorganic food as you like. Please, come this way."

***

Fenisys had wandered down the path of the deepest depths of the right, and also found himself with a spear-tip at his throat. He was certain to throw up any moment now if his stress levels did not decrease. De-escalation struck Fenisys as unlikely, however, as the man holding it eyed Fenisys with suspicion and detestation. "Another illegal refugee, huh? Here to steal our women, our jobs, and our land?"

"By no means!" Fenisys cried. "I am merely looking for food and shelter! I have coin if you'd like, and only aim to stay one night."

The man lowered his spear. "Oh, that's fine. We like visitors who spend their coin and leave. But not the ones who sneak in to work in the establishments where visitors spend their coin! They are the lowest of the low."

"But if no one can sneak in and serve the visitors, who serves them?"

The man's face went blank. "I suppose we do," he said. "By the ten hells, what horror! Waiting on others is dreary and boring!"

"My name is Fenisys. Who are you, mighty guard of this city?"

"They call me Agemedysseus," the guard said. " And you can pay for food and shelter here. It may be costly, however. Our people are starving and food is getting expensive."

"Yes, food is scarce in the Empire as well. The droughts this year have been horrific," Fenisys asked. "And the hurricanes. And the fires. And the ice kingdom to the north is melting. The great ice city of Daggergard is turning into slush. But! I am from the university! If you wish, I can show you how to grow genetically modified food."

"Ha! That garbage? You insult us by asking! It was designed by those in the city's left to cause infertility in men, so that our population would dwindle and make us easier to conquer! It is the reason their tribe bears no children. We will take no part in it! But because we do not plant it, our crops were destroyed in last summer's savage heat and we do not have food to survive the winter!"

"Oh, woe!" Fenisys cried. "Your poor people! And your poor children!"

"Alas, no child has been born to us for the last ten years," Agemedysseus said, scowling. "Our tribe requires priests to wed young lovers before they may procreate. Our last priest died years ago and no one alive knows the ancient ritual to ordain a new one. Without a priest's blessing, none may create life."

"Oh," Fenisys said. "But if you are threatened with extinction, surely you can proceed without the ritual to save yourselves."

Agemedysseus grew angry and brandished his spear. "How dare you, heathen?" he roared. "Do not question our ancient and unshakable beliefs! They are what separates us from the dangerous and unpredictable left!"

"I apologize! I will not speak of it again!"

Agemedysseus lowered his spear for good this time, still scowling. "You had better not. But you say you have coin and wish for food and shelter? So be it. Come this way and meet the tribe of the right."

Fenisys gulped. He began following Agemedysseus to the very heart of the right side of Dividika.

***

Latheck was having a marvelous time. He had all the inorganic vegan food and beer he could swallow, and was relaxing in a throne room with dozens of men and women who also worshiped the holy trinity of the far left, social justice, anti-capitalism, and climate change. "Critical race theory should be taught in kindergarten!" Latheck raved. "No, in pre-school! Mothers should be forced to listen to audiobooks on critical race theory when they are pregnant! That way, every child shall understand the heavy burden of race and racism on all manner of peoples and how it affected history! For that is what it actually is!"

Roars of approval greeted this suggestion, and glasses all around the room clinked together in celebration. "And all corporate profits should be taxed," Latheck continued. "And all excessive wealth should be taxed. And greenhouse gas emissions should be taxed. And we need a guaranteed minimum income for all people! And lots more housing! Subsidized hovel developments! That is how we will achieve prosperity! By destroying the shadowy cabal of neoliberals who secretly control the world! We shall tax them to death! For us! For our children!"

Latheck lost them with that last line. For the idea of patriarchally conceived children was a touchy subject. "I mean," Ziathian said, taking a sip of her organic beer. "Even if procreation were not patriarchal, it would be immoral from a climate change standpoint. It is deeply unethical to bring children into a world facing a global environmental catastrophe."

"Indeed," Latheck said through a mouthful of avocado. "I am voluntarily childless for much the same reasons. I have chosen a noble life of celibacy."

"I dunno," said one young man with red hair and a braided beard. "From a climate change standpoint, isn't it more ethical for us to have and raise children who value Zevren's previous climate? So they can become researchers and search for solutions? Surely the world needs new, inquisitive minds..."

Ziathian snorted. "You sound like those fools on the right. They procreate like rabbits and raise legions of uneducated hordes who believe in neither climate change nor equality."

"That is my point," the man with the braided beard said. "If we refuse to have children, shall they not conquer the Earth?"

"There are dwellers in the right of the city?" Latheck asked. "I sent my young companion there to look for food and shelter. Will he be safe among them?"

"By the wars of Jakartaria! No!" Ziathian cried, leaping to her feet. "They will mock him, subject him to their madness, accuse him of being a foreigner, and eat him alive! They have killed scores of our kin!"

Latheck leapt to his feet as well, too courageous and daring to be out-dramatized. "By the ten hells! Let us go rescue him! With my axe, we can slaughter these dogs of the right and ensure they plague this land no longer! Follow me!"

***

Fenisys had quickly learned the best way to survive among those on the right was to humour them. Once they'd decided you agreed with them, they were tremendously warm and accommodating. Fenisys had been grilled on a variety of topics once he'd been brought into the throne room, but could easily guess the answers his hosts were searching for. From his golden throne, a blond man with a braided beard burned through a few hot topics. "What is your opinion on critical race theory?"

"No person has the right to criticize any race. Especially in public schools and in our country's history classes."

Nods of approval.

"And of abortion?"

"Completely immoral. It should be banned entirely by a council of unelected, ancient wizards who arbitrarily decide the laws of Zevren from the moment they are chosen to do so until they die."

Grins and fist-pumps from the men. The women looked uneasy.

"Do you believe in the one true god? But not the desert-peoples' version?"

"Doesn't everybody?"

Slaps on the back and cheers.

"How should we aid those in poverty?"

Fenisys sensed this was a trick question and gambled on it. "Nothing. Being poor is their own fault. Our hard-earned taxes should not be used to give them comfort when they are perfectly capable of work."

Raucous applause and the stomping of feet.

"And what," the blond man asked, his voice deadly serious, "is the fairest means to tax the income of the people of Zevren?"

"A flat tax rate across the entire empire, with tax exemptions for all stocks, bonds, dividends, and inheritance," Fenisys glanced around the room, not sure if he was going quite far enough. "With the abolishment of all sales tax and corporate tax."

The blond man finally grinned. "Brother, you are truly one of us!"

Cheers and celebrations broke out among the dozens in the throne room. What food they had was offered as a generous feast, and Fenisys was offered shelter, a comfortable chair, and spirited conversation with the men. The women were nowhere in sight. After talking about sports, gladiator contests, best methods to grill steak, and why women never fucked any of them, Fenisys asked a question. "You have mentioned those on the left a few times, why is this city divided? Why do people not gather at the center?"

A wrathful silence descended on the tribe of the right. Finally, Agemedysseus spoke up. "We abandoned the center because in it we were forced to mingle with the foolish left and listen to their lies. The mainstream town criers at the center were biased and only spoke of leftist problems, like inequality, racially motivated killings by the city's guards, and climate change. We do not like talking about those things. We would rather discuss manly things like finance, our military, and personal ownership of deadly weapons. So we started our own town center, with alternate town criers who praised the empire and talked of the wicked plans the left were crafting to murder us in our beds. Once those plans were made clear, we walled ourselves off from their madness, and kill them whenever we find them in the city."

"But my mentor, my hero, the great barbarian of... lowering corporate taxes!" Fenisys ad-libbed. "He went into the left of the city! They must have him! Will they harm him?"

Agemedysseus let out a roar and drew his spear. "The left! They have cancelled many a corporate barbarian! But they shall not harm another as I draw breath! With you and your barbarian friend's aid, we shall destroy the left!"

The tribe of the right howled, grabbing their weapons and clanging swords and spears against shields. Agemedysseus climbed upon a table and addressed the horde. "Come, my brother and sisters! We shall destroy them! The left and their deep-kingdom that have been plotting against us for years! Today is the last day any of them will draw breath!"

Thus enraged, the tribe of the right charged for the city centre.

***

The two legions collided in the center of town. Not a word was spoken. Upon setting eyes on those from the other side of the city, a bloodlust consumed both sides and they began hacking madly at their foes. Armour was rent, heads rolled, swords and spears were splintered. The battle was over in a matter of minutes. All were slain, except for Agemedysseus and Ziathian, coated in the grime of war, their weapons locked, their muscles straining against the other's might. "How I'd dreamed of killing you, Agemedysseus," Ziathian said. "I used to think about it during my book club meetings."

"And I dreamed of you," Agemedysseus said through clenched teeth. "Of stabbing you deeply with my mighty blade."

"And I dreamed of straddling you and ripping that blade from your grasp."

"Foolish wench. I would never let a woman dominate me. I would have you on your hands and knees if you even tried, stabbing you from behind!"

"You would never get up from under me."

Latheck poked his head in. "Hello!" he called. "Sorry, I got lost on the way in. This city is quite the labyrinth. How was the fearsome battle?"

Fenisys also poked his head in. He made no effort to hide the fact that he'd been hiding. "O great barbarian! You are alive! There is much tension between these two groups!"

"Indeed."

Ziathian looked away from her opponent as Fenisys emerged from the gate to the right. It was the moment Agemedysseus had been waiting for. He pulled a knife from his belt and stabbed her in the heart. She let out a snarl, and swung her sword in a wild arc. Agemedysseus staggered back, gravely wounded, but remained standing. Ziathian fell, and lay among her slain kin and foes. "So," Agemedysseus said, turning to a united Latheck and Fenisys. "You are the mighty barbarian of lowering corporate taxes. I am sorry we did not meet before today."

"What?" Latheck demanded. "I am no such thing. I am a barbarian of climate change! But are there barbarians of finance? How does one become one? Does it require any schooling?"

Agemedysseus winced, and spat blood. "You are not a corporate barbarian?"

"No, but I am intrigued by the possibility. If you are looking for a corporate barbarian, I will happily become one. Tell me of the salary. Is it generous?"

Agemedysseus coughed and spat another mouthful of dark blood. The front of his shirt was soaking. "Ha. Another lie from the mighty left. What a surprise." He tried to grin, but merely grimaced in pain. "My time is short. If you are truly a barbarian of climate change, there is something you must do. A great evil lurks below this city that is the cause of the collapsing climate."

"What?" Fenisys cried. "You know what is causing this great evil? And you have not stopped it?"

"The great evil is tremendously profitable," Agemedysseus replied. "It is why Dividika exists at all. But with the city fallen, it is no longer needed. It can be stopped. There is an ancient door in the most northern part of Dividika. It will lead you to a cavern where a monster dwells. One the left and the right could not bring themselves to face, and could never destroy. Slay it, and you will end climate change. The monster's weakness is..." He paused, but had spoken his last word. He collapsed, perhaps the last of his tribe, destroyed by the brutal fighting within Dividika.

"Woe!" Latheck cried, as Agemedysseus lay face-down in a pool of blood. "If only he could have told us how to defeat this beast of climate change! Without that knowledge, there is nothing we can do! Let us return home, apprentice."

"What? No, we must have a look! We will be among the greatest of history's heroes if we end climate change! And you are a great and unstoppable barbarian warrior! Nothing can harm you! Every man or beast who challenges you is slain without hesitation! Please, Latheck, let us go have a look!"

Latheck grinned and clapped a hand on Fenisys's shoulder. "I like the way you think, young apprentice! I am an unstoppable living God, aren't I? I shall effortlessly slay this beast, just as I effortlessly slayed all opposition to social justice! Let us go!"

***

At the most northern part of the city, our heroes found a locked door. Latheck rent the lock with his axe, drawing it for the first time since they arrived, and opened the door. The door revealed a stone staircase that descended deep into the Earth. Their descent was silent. Fenisys began to tire, but Latheck did not slow down. Finally, they reached a gigantic cavern, lit by a constellation of magical rocks strewn about the ceiling. Heaps of gold and diamonds towered over Latheck and Fenisys, who gaped at the treasure in wonder. "By the ten hells," Latheck said. "This makes the Empire's treasure room look paltry! No one could spend this fortune in a hundred lifetimes!"

Fenisys approached a nearby mountain of gold and diamonds. It was so odd. The gold had not been coined or carved into anything. It was simply in chunks, the largest of which were the size of a market stall. Latheck plucked a diamond from the same pile, uncut, but larger than a toddler. "This gem alone could buy half of the Empire!"

"Does all of this belong to the monster?" Fenisys asked, turning to peer into the depths of the cavern. "Is it still here?"

His question was answered by a deep and terrifying roar that caused Latheck and Fenisys to cover their ears. They looked at each other in bewilderment. Colossal footfalls followed, which caused the mountains of treasure to tremble, sending smaller pieces cascading down their sides. The monster was headed their way. "What do we do?" Fenisys whispered, fearing once again that he would throw up.

"Hide!" Latheck grabbed his apprentice by the sleeve and pulled him behind the nearest treasure pile. Once hidden, Latheck poked his head out to watch for the approaching beast.

The nightmarish creature defied Latheck's mighty imagination.

It was a dragon. Impossibly large and entirely black from its snout to the end of its spiked tail. Gleaming red eyes looked for the intruders, and a forked tongue darted out between its fanged jaws. Its every breath was a cloud of noxious smoke. The dragon sniffed the air and looked towards the pile Latheck and Fenisys were hiding behind. "I know where you are, you fools," the dragon said in a deep, booming voice. "I can smell you. I can hear your breathing. Come out and speak to me. That is the best offer you will receive. For I can strike you down faster than you can think. What say you?"

Latheck poked his head out. "Hail, mighty dragon of Dividika! I am Latheck, the Climate Change Barbarian!"

The dragon's eyes narrowed and it bared its teeth. "Climate change?"

"I... Did I say climate change? Ha! Ha ha! I mean, I am a polyamorous, sapiosexual, 1/64th Indigenous, vegan atheist. I care nothing for climate change and am outraged by the Zevren Empire's treatment of dragons. What is your name, mighty creature?"

The fearless and malleable empathy of Latheck bought them precious seconds to live. The dragon snorted, an extra-large plume of smoke drifting from its nostrils. "I am Manchinema," the dragon said. "I am the most ancient and powerful of the dragons. I dwell in this cave and none disturb me. Why are you here?"

Fenisys finally vomited. The dragon's arrival caused his anxiety to reach critical levels, and he performed his unfortunate task behind the treasure pile. Having finally reached his limit, Fenisys felt much calmer. His anxiety could do no more to him. He grimaced and leapt from behind the treasure, facing the fearsome Manchinema. "We are here to end climate change!" Fenisys roared. "And we were told that slaying you would end the destruction of Zevren's climate! Prepare to die, monster!"

Manchinema looked at Fenisys for a moment, and then threw back his head in laughter. Each breath sent another cloud of black smoke into the air, and the monster roared with mirth until he was gasping. Manchinema grinned down at the tiny humans before him. "That was priceless. Yes, young human, slaying me would end climate change. That is common knowledge. And yet, I am an ancient and colossal dragon. Do you know why no one has tried to slay me before?"

"No," Fenisys said.

"Because slaying dragons is wrong! No one, not even dragons," Latheck shot a pleading look at Fenisys, "deserves to be persecuted in any way, shape, or form! That includes shaming or cancelling. Come, young apprentice, we clearly have no quarrel here!"

"This is why no man will slay me. Behold," Manchinema said. He squatted down where he stood. He let out a grunt, and returned to his full height. He stepped aside, and where his hindquarters had been, there was now a new pile of gold and diamonds.

"By the gods," Fenisys said.

"Yes," Manchinema said. "I eat a substance that your kind calls 'coal' and I drink what you call 'oil'. I exhale a mixture of carbon dioxide, methane, and carbon monoxide into the empire's atmosphere. I warmed the homes of Dividika. And I shit pure treasure."

"You see, young apprentice?" Latheck said. "This creature is far too lucrative to harm! Let us leave, and find other means to end climate change."

"No," Fenisys said. "We must take a stand."

But Manchinema was already growing bored. He was also hungry and thirsty and did not want to waste any time with battle. "You, barbarian," Manchinema said. "I can give you anything you wish for if you take your apprentice and leave. What do you desire?"

"I, yes, that sounds more than fair! You truly understand equality, mighty dragon!" Latheck nodded and smiled. "And I wish... I wish for immortality! I wish to be ageless and undying! For no blade to harm me! Make me an indestructible living God!"

Manchinema looked surprised. "Oh. Actually, I meant you can help yourself to some of my shit. Take as much as you want. I've got tons of it."

"You said you can give me anything I wish for," Latheck growled, drawing his axe. "Not granting my wish would be a form of oppression. It would be bigotry! Give me immortality or else!"

Manchinema hesitated. "Yes, fine. Immortality, coming right up."

Manchinema raised a scaly forepaw and waved it in the air. "It is done," Manchinema said. "You are unvanquishable."

"Excellent! Bye!" Latheck grabbed Fenisys and threw the young apprentice over his shoulder. Latheck made a beeline for the cavern's exit. Fenisys kicked and struggled against the barbarian's mighty grasp. "This isn't over!" Fenisys screamed. "I will destroy you! Stopping you is worth more than any pile of gold!"

Manchinema snorted as he turned away. "Fool. I shall endure forever."

***

Latheck did not set Fenisys down on his own two feet until they reached the centre of Dividika. Fenisys glowered at his former hero.

"What in the ten hells was that?" Fenisys growled. "Why did you abandon our quest to end climate change, when we could have defeated it once and for all?"

"Because our lives were in danger," Latheck said. "Dying would not have saved the empire."

Fenisys saw some truth to this, but he was still furious. "Well, mighty barbarian, how then shall we defeat climate change, if we will not confront that great fossil fuel consuming monster?"

"Ha!" Latheck said. "Fuck solving climate change! Did you not hear? I am immortal! I give no shits if the planet burns and if millions starve! For I will remain unvanquished! My crusades for social justice and climate change are over. For they are no longer my problem! Goodbye, apprentice. I am off to go be an unstoppable living god."

Latheck turned on his heel and left. Henceforth, he would live in comfort and luxury! Fuck trying to save the world. He did not even spare a glance at Fenisys as he strode from the town center, his footsteps fading to silence a few moments later.

Fenisys remained in the town center for some time, too demoralized to press onward. Eventually, he summoned the strength to walk towards the city's gate. After all, he saw no reason to hang around the dead city. He followed the path to the main gates. Once there, he pushed the city door open and stepped out into the sunrise. The forest fire had been tamed by the Zeven Empire's griffin-riding firefighters. The air was still thick with smoke, but Fenisys would now be able to return home. Thank goodness. He started down the path when he caught something strange out of the corner of his eye.

He stopped and craned his neck. It was Latheck. Face down in a pool of mud, unmoving. Fenisys rushed over and peeled his fallen hero from the muck. Latheck groaned, and Fenisys rolled him onto his back. "Latheck! Do you still draw breath!"

"I do. Ow. By the ten hells, that hurt."

"What did you do? Is anything broken?"

"Yes, you fool. Many things are broken. I climbed to the top of the walls and decided to try out my newfound immortality and invincibility. I aimed to leap from them and do an impressive 'superhero landing'. You know, where you land on your feet and punch the ground? A move certain to break every bone in the legs of a mortal man. Well, I did it and broke many, many bones. I am not immortal, that miserable dragon told me what I wanted to hear to save his own skin!"

"Yes, he did," Fenisys said. "He bought us off so we would not destroy him. A cunning ploy."

"Curses! If I could walk, I would return to that cavern and split his skull! Young apprentice! I am in need of aid! Help me return to Zevren for medical treatment! If you do, I shall write you a glowing reference letter and recommend you for a role in Zevren's Department of Environmental Management. You shall have a comfortable job and a pension! Please! I beg you!"

Fenisys felt no desire to help Latheck, but a cushy government job was awfully tempting. Maybe he would finally be able to afford a home. Fenisys stood next to the battered barbarian and thought for a moment. You know, he thought, I suppose I could save his life for a home and career. He grabbed the barbarian by the arms, and began dragging him back to civilization. "Thank you, sirrah!" Latheck cried. "You have proved yourself to be a mighty barbarian in your own right! For your courage, I pass the mantle of 'the Climate Change Barbarian' to you! You are no longer Fenisys, graduate student! You are Fenisys: the Climate Change Barbarian. And I shall become Latheck the Corporate Taxes Barbarian, or Latheck the Finance Barbarian in my next adventure!"

Fenisys liked the sound of his new title. Perhaps now, as a mighty barbarian, he would finally attract the interest of the maidens of Zevren. A bright future lay before him, past the destroyed forest and billowing smoke that rent the sky. Once Fenisys had dropped Latheck off at the hospital, he would seek that future out.

The Monster Encounter Support Group

Ewan finished reading his short story, *Latheck: The Climate Change Barbarian*, and put the stapled pages back in his backpack. He looked over at the group leader, Harold, for feedback. But there was no feedback to be had, for Harold's face was purple with speechless rage. In fact, Harold looked like he was going to explode. He took a deep breath and growled, "What the fuck was that?"

Ewan looked around the circle of seated group members, only now seeing that everyone around him was stone-faced. Nervousness overcame him. "That was... um... my monster story? What did you guys think?"

Tabitha gave Ewan a look of horror. "You thought this was a writers' group?"

Ewan looked around the circle of now angry faces, panic rising. "Isn't this a place for people to share their creative fiction about monsters? For feedback?"

"Oh my God!" Harold said, massaging his temples. "What is wrong with you? No! This is a support group for people who have had encounters with monsters! This is where we can talk about our run-ins with monsters without judgement! We're here to heal!"

Ewan's nervousness gave way to sheer dread. "Oh," he said. "So that's why none of you brought laptops or paper or anything."

"You seriously thought I told that embarrassing-as-fuck story about summoning a sex demon for kicks?" Tyler asked. "Dude, I bared my very soul to you. That was upsetting for me! You need to take our stories seriously!"

"Actually, I thought that was hilarious," Ewan said. "Like, kind of a perfect cautionary tale."

Tyler stood up, fists clenched. "You should leave, man. Right now."

Ewan did not need telling twice. He slung his backpack over his shoulder and was out the gym door in a matter of seconds. An uncomfortable silence fell over the group after the door shut with a painful screech. "Anyone else not going to take this seriously and be respectful?" Harold asked. "Because if so, now is the time to leave."

"No," Tabitha said. "I was telling the truth. There are cupid angels working in the store I work at. I'm sure of it. People act way too weird about the stuff they buy. It has to be cupid magic."

"But you've never seen them?" Tyler asked. "They're not flying around the store in togas or anything?"

"They're invisible."

"Sure they are."

"Hey!" Harold said. "Tyler, like I said, we need to be serious and respectful! If Tabitha says there are invisible cupids in her store coercing people into buying toasters, we accept that! We accepted everyone who is here with a monster story."

"Well, then I think the detective guy should leave," Tabitha said. "His whole thing about catching a serial killer doesn't jive with what we're doing here."

Detective Innis scowled. "A serial killer is unquestionably a monster! Monsters don't need to have fur or fangs! People can be monsters too!"

"Actually," Harold said. "I do think Tabitha has a point. This is more for supernatural incidents that our friends and family wouldn't believe. So yeah, you can stay for the rest of the meeting, but you really shouldn't be here."

Detective Innis cocked an eyebrow and smirked. "Oh really? Well, you know who might disagree with your definition of monster? The dictionary!" He pulled his phone from his pocket and brandished it like an avenging sword. "Let's have a look! Dee, dee, dee... come on, damn it... ah ha! Definition five of 'Monster' is: 'A person capable of repulsive or vile actions, or exhibiting vicious, cruel, or gruesome behaviour to the point where they are considered inhuman.' So there! Serial killers qualify as monsters and I have every right to be here!"

Detective Innis surveyed the circle, and saw he had no challengers for the moment. Harold merely glowered. "Besides," he said. "What happened to me actually happened. It was in several newspapers of record. I received a commendation. The fishiest story, if you'll pardon the brilliant and cutting witticism, is Josh's yarn about how he fornicated with a 'mermaid'."

Josh hadn't said much outside of telling his own story. At the mention of his ex, his eyes welled with tears and he began to blubber. "That happened! We were in love! And now she's gone forever!"

Tabitha reached out and put her hand on Josh's shoulder. "It's okay," she said. "It sounds like a difficult break-up. But just take it one day at a time."

"Yes, exactly," Harold said, attempting to course-correct. "I know we're all deeply traumatized—"

"I'm not," Innis said. "If anything, my encounter enhanced my capacity to enjoy literature."

"Yeah," Tyler agreed. "Like, what happened was super embarrassing, but, like, I'm pretty much over it. It's fine."

"People freaking out in my store is super weird," Tabitha said. "But it's more creepy than super traumatic or anything. I'll live with it."

"No, you're all traumatized," Harold said, crossing his arms over his chest. "Encounters with monsters are always traumatizing. They have to be."

"I can speak for my own feelings, thank you," Tabitha said, a sharpened edge creeping into her voice. "And I say that I'm fine with the cupids in my store."

"I'm sorry, but no," Harold said, shaking his head. "You're looking at this support group all wrong. See, you're supposed to agonize over bad things that happen to you and never, ever get past them or accept them. You're supposed to feel wounded and pained for the rest of your life! That's the whole point of coming here! For us to relive our pain over and over and over and realize we'll never get past it!"

"Oh," Tyler said, bewildered. "I guess I've been doing this wrong. I just wanted to vent and get it out of my system. And, you know, more on."

"Exactly," Tabitha nodded. "I just wanted to talk to people who would take me seriously. But I'm over it."

"No!" Harold stomped his foot, and shook his clenched fists in a seated, but volatile, tantrum. "The point of this is to regularly dive into our pain! And each and every one of you needs to go home and cry about what you've gone through after tonight's meeting! That's doing it properly! You all need to cry and truly feel your misery! That's how you live with the pain!"

"What if we're crying now?" Josh asked, his tears still going strong.

"I mean, I guess you don't have to, you're fine," Harold said. "But the rest of you! You all should be miserable! Like me! Because of what I went through the time I met a monster!"

"Oh yeah? And what's your monster encounter, Harold?" Tabitha asked.

Harold took a deep breath. "It's still hard for me to talk about this," he said. "But I'll try. It all started when I was a little kid, growing up in Maine. I lived in a normal suburb. My parents had decent jobs. My little brother and I used to spend a lot of time playing on a tire swing in our backyard. One evening, I was pushing him on the tire swing, seeing how high he could go. He was shrieking with delight and kept saying, 'Higher! Higher!' and I was pushing him as hard as I could.

"But something made us stop. There was a rustling in the bushes. At the edge of the backyard. Under a twisted old tree. We stopped playing on the swing and just watched the bushes for a second. Something was moving through them. My brother asked me if I thought it was a stray cat or a lost dog. I wasn't sure. But I wanted to have a look. I never thought it would be anything that could hurt me. So I went over to the bushes. Whatever it was had stopped moving. I reached out and parted a couple branches. That's when I saw it. The monster that ruined my life. A leprechaun—"

"A leprechaun?" Detective Innis asked, peering at Harold over his glasses. "That's the terrifying monster that traumatized you for life?"

"Yes!"

"Okay. Apologies. Continue."

"*Thank you*. Yes, it was a leprechaun. He froze when he saw me, and I grabbed him. I hauled him, kicking and screaming, out of the shrub and showed him to my brother. He screamed and hid behind the oak tree we'd been swinging from. I held the Leprechaun out at arm's length, holding him under the armpits. He squirmed and shouted at me, but eventually, he gave in and just glared at me. My brother came out of his hiding place, and we started asking the leprechaun questions.

"We asked him if he was magic. He said he was. We asked where he was from. He said Ireland. We asked him if he could lead us to treasure, and he went quiet. My brother asked him again, pleading with him. The leprechaun was about to answer, when our parents came outside.

"They had heard all the shouting and commotion and came out to investigate. They saw me holding the leprechaun. They were dumbstruck. My little brother had gotten too excited. He told my parents that the leprechaun might be hiding treasure somewhere. That he might tell us where it is, and that we could find it.

"My dad immediately went from concerned dad to the smooth used-car salesman that he was. He cajoled the leprechaun. Flattered him. But the leprechaun didn't budge. My dad's charm gave away to threats. He said he wouldn't let the little creature go until he told my dad where he could find treasure. Lots of it.

"The leprechaun eventually gave in. He said that there was a lake in the wilderness, way up in northern Canada. He said the lake was shaped like a fish. At the nose of the fish, there was more buried treasure than anyone could ever dream of spending. Gold, rubies, silver, diamonds! We'd be richer than anyone who'd ever lived. My dad let the leprechaun go, and took the whole family out to dinner that night.

"My parents stayed up late talking for the next couple of weeks. My dad called in sick from work and poured over maps and atlases. He found a lake shaped like a fish in the Yukon. He wanted to move to a town by the lake, so he could search for the gold. My mom didn't want to chance it. But my dad pushed and pushed and my mom eventually agreed.

"So we moved. I said goodbye to my friends at school. My parents sold the house with the tire swing. The house I grew up in. And we moved to Canada. We got a small, cold house in a dying little town.

My dad didn't even bother to look for a job. He was convinced he would find the leprechaun's gold and that we'd be set for life. My mom bought into it and bought herself a new car, all kinds of dresses, jewellery, and makeup, and bought toys for my brother and me. At first, dad was confident. He'd come home every night and say, 'It'll be tomorrow! Just you wait!' But a lot of tomorrows went by. Mum took the dresses and jewellery back. Someone came for the car and took it away.

"My dad got work on construction sites, hours away from where we lived. My mum became a manager at a grocery store. That was it. No treasure. No riches. We gave up everything for nothing. And their marriage fell apart only a couple years later! They got divorced!"

The circle was silent as Harold's story gave way to sobs. Tabitha , Taylor, Josh, and Detective Innis shared uncertain glances. Was there more? When did the really bad stuff begin? "Is that it?" Tabitha ventured.

"Yes, that's what happened. I've never gotten over it."

"Like, that sucks," Taylor said. "But, like, you're still here and seem to be doing okay."

"Don't you understand?" Tears were now running down Harold's cheeks. "We moved to another city! And never found the gold! And then my parents got divorced! And it's all the fault of that evil, monstrous leprechaun!"

"Or," Detective Innis said, "maybe your parents are just stupid."

"Stupid?" Harold roared. "What about that was stupid?"

"I mean, are they sure they had the right lake?" Innis asked. "There are something like thirty million lakes in Canada. It's possible for a couple of them to be shaped like fish. Or maybe the leprechaun was just bullshitting them. You said your dad threatened it."

"I'm telling you, my parents knew what they were doing!"

"Wait, really? That's it?" Tabitha asked. "That's your big traumatic monster encounter that you still cry about?"

"Yes! And I'm allowed to cry as much as I want! That's the point!"

"I think you just need to call your parents," Tabitha said. "This sounds like something that could be ironed out in an afternoon if everyone's willing to just talk and be open-minded."

"You don't know that!"

Before that debate could go any further, the gym doors creaked open. Everyone turned to look. Veronica, who'd told a bizarre story earlier about an instant mashed potato monster, was back from the washroom, and she was leading a newcomer to the group. "Hi everyone," she said. "Sorry I was gone for so long, I found a new guy wandering around looking for the gym. It's his first night here. Everyone, say hello to Theo."

Theo stepped, smiled, and waved. He looked very smug about something. Veronica sat back down in her seat, and Theo took an empty seat in the circle next to Harold, an enormous smile on his face. "So this is the monster support group, right?" Theo asked. "Sorry I'm so late. I got lost trying to find you guys."

"Yeah, welcome to the group," Tabitha said. "But it's only for people who have stories about supernatural encounters with monsters."

"And they need to be traumatic," Harold said, scowling at the rest of the group.

The man's grin faded a bit. "Oh. No, my story is fuckin' sweet. I went over to Europe back in January and met this smoking hot vampire woman. We hooked up and have a great thing going. I'm just back to visit my folks for a bit. And I gotta tell somebody about everything that's happened."

"Well, in that case, make yourself comfortable," Detective Innis said, perking up and smiling. "Tell us more about your crazy vampire sex odyssey."

"But—" Harold began.

"Oh, you hush up," Detective Innis said. "I want to hear this one. Pray thee, continue."

The man sat down, his grin amped back up to its original brilliance. "Alright," he said. "Check this out."

Matchmaker

I got a very strange message from Emily over ConnectPage.

Theo. Please come and get me. I am being held in Vorstden Castle in Luxembourg. The madwoman who owns the castle has been keeping me in the dungeon and I am losing my mind. Please come before she loses it completely and has me killed.

No emojis. She didn't respond to any of my replies. I was stunned to hear from Emily for two reasons. First, she's dead. Her family was informed that she died in a climbing accident in Europe a couple of months ago. Her body was never recovered. I went to her funeral. I watched them bury an empty casket. Secondly, I am her ex-boyfriend and we parted on bad terms. We broke up just before she left. So even if she were still alive somehow, I'd be the last person she would reach out to.

Still, the message was from her ConnectPage account. No reason to think it wasn't her. Are you supposed to report this kind of shit to Beta? How? It couldn't wait. I needed to find out if she was still alive and what had happened to her. I packed a bag, told work I had an emergency, and booked a seat on the next flight to Luxembourg. I brooded on the plane about what I would do when I got there. Contact the local police? Sneak into the castle and rescue her? Barge in, a knife between my teeth, and fight my way to the dungeon and to... Oh God. What was I going to do once I found her?

The more I considered my options, the more nervous I got. I ordered a whisky to calm my nerves. Then several more whiskies. By the time my nerves were settled, I wasn't sure I'd be able to stand up. But I'd come to a decision; I'd just knock on the front door of the castle and ask Emily's abductor to give her back. Maybe this woman who was holding her hostage could be reasoned with. It was worth a try.

I stepped off the plane at Luxembourg Airport and found a driver who would take me to the castle. "But I won't be waiting around for you," he said. "That place is cursed. It is ruled by a savage and heartless vampire. She eats men alive. Sucks them dry."

I still had enough alcohol in my system to manage a stoic nod as the driver said this. He gave me a worried glance in his rear-view mirror, but didn't argue. I maintained my façade of faux-bravery, and we finished the drive in silence. When we arrived, I stepped out of the car and looked up at the castle.

It was formidable. A man-made mountain of carved stone. The outer walls were scarred from barrages unleashed by ancient siege weapons. A dozen towers and turrets reached for the heavens and the main entrance could only be reached by a drawbridge across an immense moat. But the drawbridge was down and I could approach it. Still floating on liquid courage, I went up to the massive oak doors at the entrance and knocked. To my astonishment, the doors opened.

I stepped into a large hall. Great pillars held up a vaulted ceiling and the hall was lit by an immense iron chandelier. There was a golden throne flanked by a pair of sweeping staircases, which led to a second level, where a woman stood, staring down at me. She was clad in a white dress and was wearing a veil that obscured her face. "My, my," she said, in a throaty and sultry voice. "It has been quite a while since I had a visitor. Who, may I ask, dares set foot in my castle?"

"My name is Theo. I'm here to take Emily home."

"But my dear Theo," the woman began her descent down the stairs. "We haven't been properly introduced. Proper introductions are required in high society. You are Theo, and I am the great Lady Valduz. The ruler of Vorstden Castle."

"I know Emily is still alive. Tell me where she is."

"Who?" Lady Valduz asked, her tone making it perfectly clear she knew who I was asking about.

She settled into her golden throne and snapped her fingers. A gnome-like man staggered over to her and presented her with a glass of blood-red wine. Lady Valduz accepted the glass and lifted her veil, revealing aquiline features, full red lips, and yellow eyes. She took a sip of her wine and smiled. "Oh, do you mean that dreadful influencer who snuck into my castle last year? Yes, we reported her death a tad prematurely. I have not killed her yet. Although I probably should. Lord, what a pain she's been."

"Let her go. I won't ask again."

"My, my," Lady Valduz stood up and walked towards me. "Such passion. I'll have her set free immediately. I'm tired of listening to her screaming and sobbing anyhow. But you, my dear..."

She was close enough to touch and I sized her up. She was really, really tall. Like, nine or ten feet tall. Her skin was lily white. Not going to lie, she was a walking corpse. Physically dead. Not decaying at all. No blood circulation. She just didn't, frankly, look well. But! She was still hot. She had an incredible figure. Hourglass didn't come close to describing it. She must have to get all her clothes tailored. She was dazzling. She gave a sinister, yet alluring, smile and placed a hand on my shoulder. She leaned down and whispered in my ear. "Why don't you join me here? Put aside your thirst for revenge and rule by my side. I can offer you wealth, power, and pleasure beyond your wildest dreams."

She paused, her hand slipped from my shoulder and it began snaking its way down my back. "What say you to my offer?"

I'd made my mind up before she even asked. "Okay!"

Lady Valduz took a large step back and cocked her head. "I... pardon?"

"I'm in!"

"Uh..." Lady Valduz glanced around, as if to find someone to rescue her. Her gnome-butler had already vanished. "What, ah, makes you say that?"

"Are you kidding? This'll be great!" I peered around my new home, taking in the oppressive and menacing décor. "I mean, I had an office job back home. A basement apartment. It won't miss any of that. And you'll let Emily go? Seriously? Thank fuck! She can go home and that's off my to-do list. I didn't really want to see her again anyway. I just felt I had to help out, you know?"

Lady Valduz looked even more uncertain than ever and peered down at me as if I were some kind of yappy dog. But I was only getting more excited as my new situation sunk in. I was in for a life of luxury with a nine-foot-tall vampire girlfriend who was insanely hot and rich! I'd be a fool to say no! How many times in your life does an opportunity like this even come up? Lady Valduz gave me a final look-over and nodded. "Right. Okay. Well then. Would you excuse me for a moment?"

I nodded, still smiling like an idiot. I had a lot of questions for her when she came back. Would I get a crown? Could I make royal proclamations? Would we eat mutton and roast potatoes like old-fashioned nobility? Did she eat? Would she drink my blood? How good is the WIFI? Which side of the bed would be hers? There was just so much to look forward to! She turned and walked through a door off to the side of the staircase. She didn't look back once.

***

I left the stupid mortal, Theo, I think he said his name was, standing around in the throne room and began searching for the castle caretaker, Spode. I needed his advice about what on Earth I was supposed to do next.

Spode is ancient. Tiny and stooped, with a long, crooked nose and a few meagre tufts of hair that he slicks back with some kind of grease I've never been able to identify. But Spode has been looking after this castle for as long as I can remember. I've never been certain exactly what he does all day, but whenever we cross paths, I always find him up to something. I wasn't sure where he'd gotten to after he brought me my wine. I found him in the main kitchen, scrubbing a pan in soapy water. He was making very slow progress. I sat down next to him. "Spode, I think I've made a huge mistake."

"Good afternoon, m'lady. And what do you mean?"

"Well, that young mortal who came by looking for his girlfriend? That woman I've got in the dungeon? Well, I was in a theatrical mood and decided to do the whole 'join me and we shall rule together and be lovers' shtick for a lark. I figured he'd say no and then I could kill him and get on with my day. But the fucking guy actually said yes."

Spode neither looked up nor ceased scrubbing his pan. "Congratulations, m'lady. Shall I lay out the spare room for our new guest? Or will he be sharing your quarters?"

"What? No, Spode, I'm upset! I don't want this human hanging around. He thinks he's going to be making decisions around here and that we'll have sex!"

"Very good, m'lady."

"Spode! You're not listening to me! I don't want this dipshit hanging around my castle! It's mine!"

Spode stopped scrubbing his pan and looked up at me. Despite his decrepitude, his eyes hadn't lost their fierce clarity. He had the same piercing blue eyes he must have looked up at my mother with eighty years ago. He scowled and set down his scrub-brush. Suddenly, he looked exhausted. He leaned against the kitchen counter. "Did I ever tell you how I came to work at this castle?"

I'd never given it any thought. "No."

"Your mother used to feast on the local villagers, from time to time. She would sneak into the village at night and pick off a drunkard or a slattern and drink their blood. Leaving only a husk left when she was through with them."

"That sounds like the sort of thing she would do."

"I vowed to put an end to her reign of terror. I was young and fierce then. I loaded my pistol with silver bullets and sharpened a stake to run through her heart. I crept into the castle during the most terrible rainstorm. I spent hours sneaking and creeping up to her bedchamber. I found it. The door was closed and candlelight flickered under the door. I was prepared to kill her, even if it meant my death. I opened the door and saw her, sitting on her bed."

I had never heard a word of this before. I assumed Spode had always been an ancient, creaky gnome and it never occurred to me that he'd once been a hot-blooded adventurer. I leaned in. "What happened next?"

"I put the stake back in my coat pocket. Because when I saw her, she was crying. Just sitting on her bed, weeping."

"Weeping? Mother never cried."

"She was certainly crying that night. I stopped and just watched her. She was so wretched. So lonely. So instead of shooting her, or stabbing her, I just said 'hello' to her."

"What did she do?"

"She just kept on crying. She'd known I was in the castle of course. But she was too distraught to fight me or stop me."

"Why was she so upset?"

"She never said, m'lady. I never ventured to ask. We discussed other things. But I suspect it was because she was so terribly and endlessly alone. This is a large castle to wander without a friend or companion. Loneliness had broken her spirit."

I was dumbstruck. My mother, a fierce and unvanquishable woman, could never have been lonely or scared or lost. She was a warrior. A noblewoman. It simply didn't make sense. Spode must have read my expression, because he smiled. "But you never saw that side of her. Loneliness, m'lady, has a cure."

"What do you mean? What happened?"

"I sat down on the bed next to her and we talked. She talked about how empty the castle was. How she wished she had someone to share it with. How miserable she'd become. I realized that attacking the village was a cry for help. And she was reaching out in the only way she knew. Eating people. Well, no. Drinking their blood. But she'd never talked to the villagers and had no idea how to meet them. So she started eating them."

Spode smiled at the memory. He put a hand on my shoulder. "Maybe, and you'll have to forgive me m'lady, but maybe that's why you've abducted all those women over the internet. Maybe you wanted someone to come looking for them. That someone is here."

"I..."

"Take a moment, m'lady. Consider how you truly feel. What is it that you're feeling? What do you need?"

"I don't need anyone else in my life, Spode. I have you. You look after things nicely."

Spode chuckled. "I won't be around forever, m'lady. If it's not too bold of me, I would suggest you give the boy a chance. He might surprise you."

I sat for a moment and thought about how I'd been feeling. I'd been lonely. Part of me wanted a friend, or a companion, around. Could that be Theo? He seemed kind of dopey. But loyal. And determined. I mean... I suppose I could give him a trial run...

I stood up. "I think I'll go chat with Theo."

"Very good m'lady. I shall prepare a tower bedroom for him."

I started back towards the throne room where Theo was, but stopped just outside the door. Actually, I could check in with Emily, the influencer in the dungeon, and ask her about Theo. She could be a character reference. If she painted a damning picture, I could eat him. If she painted him as a decent guy, I'd let him stay awhile and see how we get on. But I had a precious resource in my dungeon, and I'd be a fool not to use it. Plus, it was time to let her go anyway. So, I descended the stairs to the dungeon and went to chat with my captive.

I found her in her cell, reading in her bed. Yes, she has a feather bed, a stack of books, Netflix, and Spode brings her anything she wants to eat. I took her phone and gave it to Spode. But she has anything else she can ask for. She's costing me a small fortune. I'm not a monster, damnit. Just a vampire. And she broke into my castle. So why not have some fun with her? I'd passed some boring evenings threatening to eat her or to turn her into a ghoul, but she gave me a lot of attitude. She never begged for mercy or grovelled. She just called me a bitch and a monster and eventually I just stopped visiting her. But now I had something of hers. This time I wondered if I could get to her. "Someone is here for you," I said, stepping up to the bars of her cell door. "Someone has come to rescue you."

She sighed in annoyance and marked her place in the book. Obama's memoir, incidentally. She was committed to reading the entire thing. She turned and looked at me with disdain. "What, are you messing with me again? If you're going to bullshit me, just get out."

"I am telling the truth. A man is here for you. Theo, I think his name is."

She leapt up from her bed. "He is? Where is he? Have you harmed him?"

"No. I offered him a chance to fuck my brains out, live in my castle, and rule by my side."

"What? What did he say to that?"

"He said yes."

"What?! That... fuckhead! I shouldn't even be surprised! Fuck him!"

Uh oh. "Why do you say that?"

85

"Oh please!" She looked me over, her venomous expression crossing over to a murderous one. "You're this nine-foot-tall, slutty immortal vampire chick with huge boobs! He's a fucking administrative assistant, and he has a thing for older women! Of course he said yes! You can actually tell him about living through World War Two. He'll love that. He's a dopey, horny little man and he'd say yes to anyone that might fuck him some day! I'm not fucking surprised. I'm just disappointed. He's still... so... Theo. That dipshit."

"He must have some redeeming qualities," I offered.

Emily's bloodthirsty expression softened. "He's... very loyal. Very considerate. And committed. He was always very generous to his friends. And he was so good with my parents. He just put them at ease, you know?"

"So a good man, then?"

"Yeah. Like, dopey, but a good guy."

So far, so good. I struggled for a moment to find a way to make my next question sound casual. "And what was he like in bed?"

"Like I said, he's very considerate. And he... wait, are you seriously going to hook up with him? And turn him into your live-in sex slave and housekeeper or something?"

I liked the sound of that. "Precisely. And you say he does admin work? Like ordering office supplies and answering emails?"

"Yeah..."

Well, he could do all that for me too. I was starting to come around to the idea. Spode could still... cook for himself... and clean. Whatever it is he does. Perhaps Theo could handle the more mundane parts of ruling over a castle I found dreary. Emily continued to glare at me, and I smiled at her. "Anyway, I really am setting you free. Theo will be much nicer company than you ever were."

"I was your slave, you bitch."

"Oh please. You've practically had an all-inclusive vacation. I'm unlocking your cell now. Take the stairs to the hall and then take a left. You'll see the main hall and can leave out the main gate."

"Where's Theo?"

"He's waiting for me in the main hall."

Emily pushed through her unlocked cell door and made a beeline for the stairs. "I'll fucking kill him."

"No, you won't," I said, following her. "If you hurt my new boytoy, well, potential boytoy, I will eat you."

"I'd like to see you try, bitch."

***

"Master Theo?"

I turned around to see the ancient gnome-man standing near a wooden door on the far side of the hall. He offered me a pained and brief bow. "My name is Spode. I am the castle caretaker and Lady Valduz's servant. I understand you will be Lady Valduz's guest. If you'll follow me, sir, I'll show you to your room."

"Oh, sure."

"Do you have any luggage, Master Theo?"

"Um. No. Just this bag. I didn't think I'd be staying."

"No matter. Follow me, please."

I followed Spode through a maze of hallways and spiral staircases. One hallway was covered in tapestries. One had suits of armour. The walls of the third hallway were adorned with mediaeval weapons. I tried to memorize it so I could find my way back downstairs, but I gave up quickly. This was going to take time to figure out. "Spode?"

"Yes, Master Theo?"

"I hope this isn't rude or anything, but Lady Valduz is really hot."

"As you say, Master Theo."

"So... what's the plan now? Am I just going to be a kept man? Because that's totally fine. I have no issues with that."

"I suspect that Lady Valduz will find something for you to do around the castle. The young men who venture here are usually put to work."

"Oh... do lots of young guys come and go around here?"

"No, Master Theo. I was only referring to you and myself. But whatever skillset you possess, Lady Valduz will ask you to use it to pitch in. Keeping up a castle is a great deal of work."

"Oh. Cool."

***

I followed Emily into the main hall, but when we got there, there was no trace of Theo. At the sight of the abandoned hall, Emily whirled around. "Where is he? What have you done with him?"

Holding someone captive makes them distrustful of you, and a tad paranoid. I scowled and glared down at her. "I left him here to wait for me. I don't know where he is. But I'm confident he is already at work in this castle, serving me with the utmost devotion."

In truth, I was far less certain. I'd been quite dismissive towards him earlier. Maybe he had second thoughts and took off. The possibility worried me. I had been looking forward to at least talking to him again. But I tried not to let that show. "You have no more business here," I said. "Begone! Before I change my mind and feast on your blood!"

"Fine! But you tell Theo he's a sack of shit and if I could do it all again, I'd never have sucked his dick in that hot tub the night we met! I'd have ignored him, and I'd have actually enjoyed my twenties instead! Tell him to get fucked!"

With that, she stormed over to the entrance, pulled open the oak doors, and left.

With her gone (thank goodness), I needed to find Theo or Spode. I went over to my throne and rang the bell. I gave it a minute. Silence. Spode must have been in the upper castle. Out of earshot. He might be settling Theo into one of the towers. I could easily see for myself if that was the case.

Being a vampire has several advantages. Eternal life and beauty. I don't need sleep. Or food. Well, blood. Pig blood does nicely. Only drama queens hunt people. Also, I can turn into a bat and fly around. Which I have grown to find incredibly useful. Given the size of the castle and our lack of elevator, if I need to get to another part of the castle in a hurry, I transform into a bat, fly out the nearest window, soar over the castle, and fly into a window closer to where I need to be.

As I do this frequently, I have a rule that all the windows in the castle are to be left unlocked. That way, I can just fly in the window, or push it open in bat form and fly right in. Spode, however, is mindful of people potentially breaking in, having once done so himself with the intent to murder everyone inside, so he frequently closes and locks them.

So I flew to the nicest tower bedroom, where I figured Spode was helping Theo settle in. I soared above the tower, and then dove for the window, hoping to make an elegant and spooky entrance. But that did not happen. Instead, I collided with the closed window with a dull "thud" that rattled my bones. I was stuck to the side of the window, pressed against the glass, pain radiating from my every nerve ending. Theo and Spode looked over at the window. Theo looked nervous and Spode looked alarmed. "Oh dear!" Spode hobbled over to the window and unlocked it. "Your ladyship! Apologies!"

Spode peeled me off the outside of the glass and set me on the bed. I lay there for a moment, stunned and unable to move. Once I regained my senses, I took a deep breath and focused on transforming back into a vampire. I felt my skin bubble and stretch. My bones groaned and shifted. It isn't painful, but I'm told it is unsettling to watch. Spode, as stoic as he is, usually looks away. Actually, that little matchmaker covered for me, and showed Theo the view out the window while I transformed. Very thoughtful.

Once I'd finished, I rose from the bed. Spode turned around and gave Theo a tap on the shoulder. Theo turned around and looked up at me. He looked a touch nervous, now that he was sobering up and we were face-to-face. "Hello Theo," I said. "I see Spode is showing you your quarters. Is everything in order?"

"Yes, m'lady," Spode said, not trusting Theo to speak. "We will have to get clothes and essentials for our guest. He was not expecting to stay with us long."

"Theo, make a list of what you need. We will have it delivered. Everything comes from the Amazons now. Spode contacts them through the computer. Their people do not fail us."

"Very good, m'lady. Master Theo can bring the list to me in the kitchen. I will get back to the washing up."

I suspected the washing up was already done and that Spode was just trying to leave us alone together. Spode gave me a look that said, *play nice*, and he left, closing the door behind him. Theo gave me a shy smile that would have warmed my heart if it were still beating. "Do you... like the *Matrix* films, my lady?"

He called me *my lady*. How cute. "Um. I am not sure. Which films are those?"

"The ones starring Keanu Reeves. The first one is a classic. Have you ever seen it? Would you like to?"

"I could be persuaded. Does it have a happy ending?"

Theo considered this. "Mostly."

"Then I shall try it."

Theo smiled again.

"Well," I said. "You can freshen up with what is already here for you. And after that, you can get caught up on mail, correspondence, bills, all that sort of thing. You will earn your keep in my castle, and I understand those are your skills."

"Yes," Theo said, relieved not to have to do hard labour or clean the moat. "That's no problem."

"Do you have any questions? Is there anything you need?"

"Yeah, does this place have WIFI? And what's the password? Can I listen to my podcasts while I sort the mail?"

"Oh... yes, I have it written down somewhere... I'll have to look for it. But yes, knock yourself out. Our internet is yours. We have as much of it as we want."

Theo nodded, still smiling. He opened his mouth to speak, but hesitated. He gathered his courage and gave it one more try. "It's very nice to meet you, Lady Valduz," he said. "I look forward to getting to know you more. Will we be able to have dinner together tonight?"

Adorable. Dopey, to be sure. But like Emily said, loyal, dependable, and a good guy. I suppressed a smile and turned to leave. "Yes, dinner is at seven. Looking forward to it."

Theo nodded.

"Oh, and Theo," I called over my shoulder. "After dinner... I suppose I'll need a massage and help getting out of my corset. I hope you'll be agreeable to helping me with that sort of thing."

I didn't look back at him, but from the tone of his "Yes, your ladyship!", I bet he was grinning from ear-to-ear.

***

Spode and I were waiting for Theo at the kitchen table. He'd been living with me for a year. We'd been happy. He'd gotten some peasant in the village to reforge somebody's gold tooth into a ring. He gave it to me in August. Currently, he is late for dinner. Presumed lost. Dumb, but loyal. In fairness, we share a truly gigantic castle. Spode was in a chatty mood. "My ladyship, does Theo's courtship mean you will no longer have me following young women on ClickSnap and luring them into your dungeon?"

"I... why do you bring that up?"

"It is among the last of my duties, madam. But one I haven't done in some time now. Otherwise, Theo has taken over for me entirely. The castle is in good order."

"I am glad. Yes, um, no more abducting influencers. I can manage without them. Thank you, Spode."

"Oh, don't mention it, m'lady. 'Tis not hard to manage a castle. I've always liked the peace and quiet, and I've had plenty of time to read."

"You're welcome to stay as long as you like. I have no doubt you are still the adventurer who scaled the castle wall eighty years ago"

"That is very kind of you, Katerina. No, I will remain amongst these halls until I join your mother once and for all."

"I'm sure she'll be delighted to see you."

"As I, her."

There was a moment's silence. As there can only be between old friends who are at ease with one another. "By the way," Spode said. "I do think he's a catch."

"I am fortunate he sought out my castle."

"M'lady, it was no turn of fate. I messaged him."

"What?"

"I took all of your captives' phones. I went through them. I could ensure the right people were contacted so as to not draw attention to any of your victims' disappearances. But Theo, I thought, was a fine young man to reach out to."

"Spode! You were pimping me out!"

"I merely sent a message for help, m'lady. Anything could have happened. You could have eaten him. But I suspected you would not."

"Don't rule it out entirely. My glass of blood is getting cold."

"Would you like me to heat it up, m'lady?"

"No. It'll give me something to complain about whenever Theo gets here. Leave it be."

The Sound and the Furry

Joy bloomed in Hosanna's heart as she heard the laughter, chatter, squeals of delight, and animal sounds made by dozens, no, hundreds of happy people. People like her, who were outsiders and needed a place to feel safe and loved. A place away from prying eyes and judgement. A safe space to truly be oneself and to forget, if only for a single afternoon, what the rest of the world might think. For the first time in her life, she felt at home.

She was also starting to feel awfully warm. Because she was wearing an elaborate furry costume. It was pink and white, with enormous anime-eyes, a dazed expression, and an uptilted tail. Everyone around Hosanna was wearing furry costumes, actually. Because Hosanna had just set foot in "Unleash the Furry 2023", a three-day convention exclusively for furries.

What are furries, you may be asking? Well, they are members of a subculture that have a deep and abiding affection for anthropomorphic animals. They like to do roleplaying games under their assumed furry identities, or 'fursonas'. They like to make arts and crafts, including lots of drawings of human-animal hybrids having vicious, borderline-psychotic sex. Which is not to say that all furry art is pornographic, but lots of it is. They also like to make or buy anime-style furry costumes and hang out at conventions.

The conventions are meant to be good, clean fun. In fur costumes. A chance to unwind. In fur costumes. To buy furry art and memorabilia. Still in fur costumes. But despite the furries' peaceful and playful intentions, the attendees of this convention were scaring the fuck out of the two-hundred odd Afghan refugees who were also sharing the hotel the furries had all booked. The Afghans (wisely, as it would turn out) mostly hid in their rooms and waited for the demonic fur people to leave. They would not have to wait very long, as tragedy was already brewing.

But for the moment, Hosanna was overjoyed. She was among her people. She was warm and toasty. It was heaven. She hardly noticed the bang of a door being torn open on the other side of the convention centre. She was too busy looking at furry art to hear the gasps and cries of alarm as a phalanx of creatures swarmed the astonished furries. Hosanna only realized something was wrong once the screaming started.

Panic and chaos followed. Furries ran, half-blinded by their costume masks and half-blinded by fear. The terrified furries collided with concrete walls, smashed into market stalls, and stumbled over dropped purchases. They were easy prey for their attackers. Hosanna, fearful that she would never reach the exit, dove under a table. She was hidden by a long black tablecloth and made no sound. She heard further screams. The snapping of powerful jaws that had clamped upon a slow-moving target. Fabric ripping. Pleas for mercy. Snarls. Howls. Gruesome laughter. Then silence.

Hosanna wondered if now was her chance to make a break for it. Perhaps the attackers had left. She was about to lift the tablecloth to escape when she heard the heavy footfalls of the hunters' paws.

A monster called out to another in a guttural, growling voice. "Ripper. Come have a look at this."

"What is it? I... Oh, shit."

"They're not werewolves. They're humans in costumes."

"Fuck."

"This is bad. When the human leaders see this, they'll realize we've violated the treaty."

A third monster voice called over. "Why are you two stalling? Get back with the wolfpack."

"Howler. You need to see this."

"No, we need to catch up with the pack and... Oh goddamn it. They're people, aren't they?"

"Looks like it."

93

"What the fuck are they even doing?"

"No idea. These are ceremonial winter coats of some kind."

"Perhaps they were worshipping us."

"It doesn't matter. No humans can live to speak of this. Look for the rest. Kill everything. If a single human escapes, it will be the end of our way of life."

Hosanna panicked. It was now or never, she crawled from her hiding place and threw up her hands. "Wait! Stop! I promise not to breathe a word!"

She looked at the monsters standing before her. Three massive, bloody werewolves. They turned and looked at her. They were huge creatures. Canine, furry, wrathful, but poised. And, oh my goodness, they were absolutely jacked. Just ripped. Like something out of *Men's Health*. But with fur. *Damn*. Hosanna's terror gave way to intrigue. She did, after all, like big strong men in fur costumes. Actual werewolves were fine too. This day could still turn around, she thought. "If you promise not to hurt anyone else," Hosanna said, "I will help you escape and cover this up. Please!"

The werewolves looked at each other, uncertain and skeptical. The largest of the three, a grey and battle-scarred alpha, stepped forward. "And why should we do that?"

"I'll help you cover this up," Hosanna said. "This was all just a misunderstanding, right? You get rid of the bodies, I'll tell everyone this was all just a prank or something. It'll blow over."

The alpha snorted. "You think your race stupid enough to believe such an obvious lie?"

"Oh, that's not even a question. It'll be fine. If you spare me, no, wait! If you take me with you, I will solve this for you!"

The alpha considered this. "Who are you to be so bold and to speak for the human race? Are you the queen of these fur-wearing people?"

Pause.

Well... Why not?

"I am."

The alpha nodded. "That explains your confidence. Tell your subjects that all is well. We shall remove the slain. Once you have calmed your people, join us outside. You may run with us, queen of the fur people."

"Oh yes!" Hosanna could just imagine it. Frolicking in meadows. Cuddling up against a hairy version of The Rock to pass a winter evening. Meals of berries, kale, and toasted oats! "I'll be right back!"

Hosanna sprinted to the reception area of the convention centre. Dozens of furries were gathered there, their suspicions raised only in faint, whispered fear:

"What even happened in there, man?"

"Is this some kind of viral marketing thing? Like, is this going to be all over social media?"

"This always happens! Last time I went to Unleash the Furry, someone tried to gas the convention centre!"

Hosanna climbed up onto a table and waved her arms. "Can I have everyone's attention?"

People turned to look. They were starved for information and direction. For the most part, they waited quietly.

Hosanna tried to sound jovial. "To all the attendees of 'Unleash the Furry 2023', the *practical joke* is over and it was hilarious. We invite all attendees to return to the convention centre to get back to our scheduled events and celebrations! It is safe to do so, and we would love to see you there."

"Practical joke?"

"Oh, like a Logan Paul thing! Ha!"

"I knew it was a viral marketing thing!"

"Come my brethren! Let us return to the halls of our people and yiff!"

The crowd turned and went back into the convention hall. Wow, controlling the masses is easy, Hosanna thought. All it takes is some gentle directions and they'll go where you want on their own. The reassured furries soon returned to their festivities, the corpses removed and (most) of the blood having been licked off the floor. Everything returned to a familiar rhythm. Even the broken doors had been more-or-less jammed into place. Hosanna slipped away from the crowds and ventured into the nearby forest. She followed a single track of werewolf footprints in the snow, which led her to the waiting wolfpack. There were perhaps two-dozen of them. Male and female.

They surrounded her, sniffing the air, but were otherwise silent. "You handled that well," the alpha wolf said. "You are truly a mighty queen and you are welcome to run with us."

"I'd be honoured."

"It is a hard life. But it will make you strong and you will forge bonds with the wolfpack that will never be broken. But be warned; many among the wolfpack will vie for your companionship."

Okay! Hosanna only seemed to fully take in that last part. And she was thrilled. While she neither created nor consumed (hardcore) furry porn, the hairy, eloquent, muscular werewolves that surrounded her were thrilling and exotic. She was looking forward to being courted, and to cuddly, snuggly sessions with werewolf men. Her fantasies were interrupted by orders from the alpha. "We move north," he said. "Let us find new prey."

The werewolves howled their agreement, and they loped off into the depths of the forest without a look back. Hosanna was left standing alone. A sense of overwhelming dread consumed her as she realized how much exercise this new life would entail. Hosanna hadn't run since grade school. Her exercise regimen started and stopped at an occasional walk in the park near her house. In fact, wandering the park was one of the very few reasons she ever left her home. This furry convention was the first time she'd been around people since Christmas.

However, the thrill of life among werewolves was too much to pass up. Even if it meant having to do cardio. Hosanna took a deep breath and set off at a jog after her new companions, following their tracks in the snow.

Hosanna gave up jogging after a few minutes and power-walked through the forest. It took over an hour, but she eventually reconnected with the wolfpack, who were feeding on an unlucky deer. The werewolves' snouts were covered in blood. There was not enough deer for everyone, and there was some snapping and snarling over who got to eat first. The more cowardly werewolves sat back, making sad puppy dog eyes at those who were feasting. Hosanna sat on a log at the edge of the group, watching, hoping someone would make her a fruit salad or get her some nuts. No such luck. One white and brown werewolf did notice her, and brought her a lump of raw meat. "Here, human," he said. "Eat this to recover your strength. We have more ground to cover tonight."

Great. Hosanna looked at the handful of flesh she'd been given and wondered if she could find some wild rosemary or oregano in the forest to season it with. She hadn't eaten meat in years. Still, she removed the head of her fursuit, and set it next to her. A few wolves looked over. She smiled and waved, and began to chew the hunk of meat. It went down okay. She got up and sat closer to the wolves. Several came over and sniffed her. A powerful-looking one nuzzled her for a few precious moments. This is it, Hosanna thought. I've just met my furry protector and provider. Yes please.

Except no. The cuddly, macho werewolf moved on and began snuggling with a female of his own kind. But two other werewolves approached Hosanna. They were not rugged or muscular like the alpha and betas. Rather, they were scrawny and awkward, and seemed uncomfortable and uncertain in their own bodies. These unimpressive omega wolves sat down with Hosanna. The ganglier of the two made the introductions. "My name is Tame," he said. "And this is my buddy Mange."

Mange nodded, giving Hosanna a single shy look before fixing his gaze on the ground, where it remained for the rest of the conversation. "So, you're, like, a human?" Tame asked. "That's really cool. I'm really into human stuff."

"Thanks. I really love animals too. Especially wolves and foxes."

"Oh, that's cool."

There was an uncertain silence. Mange chimed in. "I've always thought humans were hot. Kind of mysterious and wild."

"Same," Tame agreed. "But lots of members of the wolfpack think we're weird for being into humans."

"It's not weird at all," Hosanna said, giving the rest of the wolfpack a searing glare. "The rest of your wolfpack can stuff their gender norms, social norms, and species norms up their asses! You're not weird, you're enlightened."

Tame and Mange looked grateful to hear this. Tame was working up the courage to say something else when the alpha rose to his feet and made an announcement. "Time to move. We need to reach safe territory by nightfall."

The wolfpack howled in agreement. The alpha took off into the wilderness, and the werewolves followed. Tame and Mange managed pathetic howls of their own, and loped off at the tail-end of the pack. Hosanna put the head of her fursuit on, and ran after them.

***

Hosanna grew strong over the coming weeks. Her body was whittled down to a lean and athletic frame. Her fursuit grew so worn and tattered that it was little more than a grimy rag draped over her body. She howled with the wolfpack at the alpha's orders, and became an accepted member of the pack.

However, Hosanna grew a little bit pissed that the only werewolves who expressed interest in her were the deeply insecure and socially awkward ones. She watched with envy as female werewolves with luscious coats and mischievous eyes were courted by the alpha, or were fought over by betas vying for mating rights. Hosanna's two omega suitors, meanwhile, sat at a distance from her and just engaged her in banal conversation:

"So, what's your favourite kind of tree?"

"Why do humans wear cloth hooves over their feet?"

"Do you want to have cubs someday?"

Hosanna wanted Tame and Mange to ask her things like, 'do you want to snuggle?' or 'can we sneak off somewhere to be alone?', but the omegas were too clueless to ask. During a question session about where Hosanna preferred to drink from creeks, rivers, brooks, or puddles, she finally got fed up and stood up, turning to glare down at Tame and Mange. "I did not come all the way into the wilderness to answer stupid get-to-know-you questions! I am here to be free from society and to be protected by a powerful, fierce, dominant werewolf; while remaining an empowered and independent feminist! I've had enough of you two!"

Mange scrambled to his feet. "Wait!" he cried. "I can be that werewolf!"

Tame stepped in front of him. "I feel like we really connect. I can be that wolf for you. Please."

Hosanna was struck by an idea. With one simple request, she could have everything she wanted. She could be fought over. She could have a champion. She could be a prize to be won. "You have

98

to fight each other for my hand," Hosanna said. "You must draw blood. The winner will have me."

Tame and Mange both looked terrified at the idea. Mange swallowed. "I really, really like you. Like, a lot. I can fight if you really want me to. But if we can, you know, talk this out. That would be okay too."

Tame nodded. "Hosanna, I think you're really special. Like, conversation is a way better way to solve most problems. You know? But I can fight if you want me to."

"I do," Hosanna said. "So get to it."

The rest of the wolfpack had gathered, spellbound. Omegas rarely fought, and the alphas and betas were curious to see how the duel between such pathetic warriors would unfold.

Tame and Mange stood and faced each other, now surrounded by the wolfpack. Hosanna stood to the side, and gave a single nod.

It was time to begin.

Tame struck first. In a sense. He screwed up his eyes in terror and threw a hopeless punch at Mange. Mange, too frightened by the fist speeding towards his awaiting face to move, took the blow right between the eyes and was sent reeling. Tame also cried out in pain, as his punch was so poorly delivered that it injured his paw. Tame cradled his paw to his chest, shooting a desperate look at Hosanna. Hosanna simply smiled. Mange recovered his footing, determined to strike back. Mange's punches were no better than Tame's, so Mange did the one ancient move sure to strike at the core of his opponent. He kicked Tame in the balls as hard as he possibly could. Tame let out a shriek that echoed for miles and doubled over. By sheer dumb luck, Tame headbutted Mange in the face while doing so, sending Mange to his elbows and knees, too dazed to stand back up. Tame's terror finally gave way to fury. It dulled his agony, allowing a reinvigorated Tame to charge at Mange, colliding with him and knocking them both to the ground.

However, Tame hit his head on a log and Mange collided with a large rock. The impact from both collisions absorbed what little fight both warriors had left. Both lay on the ground, awash in pain, unmoving. Hosanna was furious. "One of you get up! I need a champion."

Tame whimpered and curled up into a ball. Mange, fairing slightly better, took a feeble swing at Tame with his claws and scratched Tame's shoulder. A few drops of blood escaped from the wound. Tame's whimpering intensified and Mange crawled away from him. "I drew blood," Mange said, crawling to Hosanna. "Can we stop now?"

"I forfeit, if that means this can be over," Tame offered, too pained and humiliated to move.

"Yeah. Fine," Hosanna said. "Just so you know, that was so weak. You both have claws! And sharp teeth! You could have fought to the death! Why didn't you take this seriously?"

"Tame is my buddy," Mange said. "I'd never kill him!"

"Aw, thanks man," Tame said, struggling to his feet. "I feel the same way."

Mange saw his friend struggling, and held out a paw. Tame accepted, and Mange pulled him to his feet. The two omegas did something unexpected. They hugged. An unabashed, eyes-closed, grateful bro-hug in front of everyone. The alpha and beta wolves began to laugh. "That was the most pathetic fight I've ever seen," the alpha said. "It was priceless!"

Hosanna's anger grew like a wildfire. "Um, hello! Mange! You just won my hand! You're supposed to be hugging me! Not him!"

Mange didn't open his eyes or move to leave the hug. "You made me hurt my best friend. Just give me a minute here."

Hosanna's fury boiled over. "What the fuck? What is wrong with you two? Hell, what is wrong with all of you? I am hot! I am exotic! Why are only the most pathetic of you fighting over me? I am a thoughtful, romantic, passionate individual and I should be seen as such!"

"Yes, you are a strong member of the pack," the alpha said. "But you're human. Plain and simple."

"And what does that have to do with anything?" Hosanna asked.

"Well, most werewolves just aren't into humans," The alpha said. Many betas nodded. "Just like most humans aren't into werewolves. Tell me honestly, how many people can you name that have romantic fantasies about monsters?"

"Dozens! I personally know dozens of furries just like me! And that's not counting the hundreds of thousands on Reddit! People who dream of escaping the human world! Who dreams of finding solace in the muscular and hairy arms of a werewolf, or wendigo, or something!"

"Well, you're extremely biased," the alpha said. "You seek out your kind on the internet to feel validated, yes? The internet, an anonymous hive-mind of billions, is how you found your people and learned of the convention we found you at. But I assure you, most humans would find your fixations... unusual."

"It doesn't matter how small, or niche, or scattered my people are! We are what we are! And screw you if you're not open-minded enough to embrace it!"

The alpha shrugged. "You have two suitors. Yet, you seem to think you're better than them. You must honour your agreement to take the winner, or leave the pack forever!"

"Fine!" Hosanna screamed. "That's fine! I'll leave! I'll go back to the human world! Back on the internet! I'll find a man, a real man, who's a furry, who has a job, and who doesn't make me run ten miles every day!"

The alpha nodded. "So be it. It was an honour to run with you, human."

Mange and Tame finally ended their hug. "Wait, seriously?" Mange asked. "You're just going to leave?"

Hosanna felt a twinge of regret. Mange was pathetic, but he was her wolf. "I'm sorry, but I need to be somewhere where I'm accepted. I think I need to go back."

Mange nodded, eyes downcast. Much like their first conversation. "Okay. Well, it was nice to meet a human. You're pretty cool."

While that was wide-open to debate, it cheered Hosanna to hear it. Yes, she thought. I am pretty cool. In fact, her time with the wolves could make her the coolest person in her furry forum chats and art communities! She had some great stories to tell, if nothing else. Hosanna said her goodbyes, gave Mange a hug, and began the long trek back to civilization.

Tame and Mange watched her go.

"Hey, can I ask you something?"

"Of course!"

"Did you ever think about... doing things with her?"

"No, not really, to be honest. That would be weird. I just hoped it would be a platonic kind of thing."

"Yeah, same."

The alpha snorted. "Bullshit. You two were desperate. You'd have done whatever she asked if she'd stuck around. Wimps."

Tame and Mange made no argument. But they had, at least, convinced each other. That was enough. And they were perfectly content to drop the subject forever. Thankfully, the alpha was also keen to move on. He turned to the wolfpack. "Let us hunt!"

Hosanna heard the wolfpack's howls for the last time and she ran towards civilization. She had a single moment where she considered turning back to rejoin the pack, but decided against it. She let out a werewolf howl of her own, without stopping or slowing her pace. She thought she heard a mournful howl in return, but it was over too quickly to be certain. Hosanna ran though the woods, towards civilization, wondering if she would ever howl for the werewolves again.

The Monster Encounter Support Group II

"That is some seriously crazy shit," Tyler said, picking up his beer bottle, hoping to find a final sip. "So how have you found readjusting to civilization?"

"Pretty easy, actually," Hosanna said. "Being able to just buy food whenever I want, and access to clean water and toilets is the best. And internet! God, I missed the internet. I'm amazed I ran with the werewolves as long as I did."

"Have you been to any more furry conventions since then?" Detective Innis asked. "Are there any coming up around here? Where can I, hypothetically, buy a fursuit?"

Hosanna shook her head. "People are pretty scared to gather like that these days. A few conventions since then have been attacked by werewolves. It's turning into a real problem. I wouldn't rush out and get a fursuit right now, unless you want to stay toasty-warm at home!"

Detective Innis looked to be considering it. Theo just nodded. "The castle Lady Valduz and I live in does get super cold and drafty sometimes. Maybe not a fursuit, but I should buy some warm clothes while I'm in town."

Detective Innis changed gears, turning his attention back to Theo. "Say. Do you have any pictures of your vampire woman? Anything, maybe, in the 'hidden' section of your phone?"

"I mean, yeah," Theo said. "But she's invisible in all of them. Like, you can't photograph a vampire. Even digitally. So the naked pictures don't do her justice. Not that I would show them to you."

"Such a shame," Detective Innis said, taking a sip of his second beer. The support group's meeting had ended with Harold stomping off in a fit of cold fury after Theo's romantic tale, so our storytellers

103

had continued onwards to a nearby bar where they could dive into the weirder and wackier sorts of stories that Harold disapproved of. A small crowd had gathered around the storytellers to listen, and now that Hosanna's tale was over, the crowd went to the bar to reload. Innis polished off his drink and smiled. "Well, this is refreshing, ladies and gentlemen. Much nicer than meeting in a stuffy old gym. Does anyone else have any good monster stories? Anyone else see any supernatural occurrences?"

"My buddy fucked a mermaid!"

"Oh, just shut up, Mike!" cried the volunteer's wife.

"I got one," said one nearby man with a ponytail and a goatee. "You ever hear about that old rock band, The How? They had some hits in the 60's. 'Tabletop Wizard' and 'This Generation'."

"Oh yeah," Tyler said. "I've listened to their stuff. Saw a couple of the surviving guys in concert years ago."

"Well, they're still going," the man said. "Well, as much as one fourth of them can go. I was part of the road crew for their last tour. Did you guys hear about it?"

"Uh, no."

"They were touring again?"

"Who?"

The man nodded. "Yeah, they went back on tour a couple years ago, and they pulled some freaky supernatural shit during the tour. Like, there was literally a portal to Hell open backstage. And that's not even the craziest part of the tour."

"That's nothing," a woman with an elaborate cocktail replied. "I do sales and marketing at ConnectPage. We changed our name to Beta recently, but it's the same shit. But you wouldn't believe the insane shit that can happen in our offices."

"Oh, like how they're rigging elections and encouraging people to plan genocides and shit?" Theo asked. "Yeah, that's been in the news."

"No," the woman said. "I mean, crazy shit aside from that. There's something seriously evil going on there."

"Anything supernatural?" Tyler asked.

She thought about it for a moment. "Maybe. There's definitely something in the office that isn't alive. Like, I've never seen it or heard it," she said. "But it's making all the decisions and controlling everything. But I don't think it's a ghost or a poltergeist or any of that shit. I think it's something someone in the company made. Something terrible. I think it's starting to make people go crazy."

Detective Innis snorted. "That is merely the effects of social media on the human brain."

"No. I think it goes deeper than that."

"There's this one woman in my yoga class who found a magic lamp at the gym," offered a handsome woman who did not look away from her phone.

Tyler rolled his eyes. This woman, Amanda, had been trying to talk them all into investing in cryptocurrencies in between stories earlier. He wasn't prepared to take her seriously. "Let me guess, there was a genie in it?"

"I don't know," Amanada did not look up from her screen. "But since she found it, her husband has gotten way hotter and she's way more successful in life. Something supernatural is up with her. And it's made her a total bitch."

Both storytellers and listeners drifted back to the table with fresh drinks. An expectant silence settled over the crowd. "Who's next?" Detective Innis asked.

The roadie raised his hand. "Yeah. Okay. So, here's what I saw on this show I worked on last summer..."

Long Live Rock!

"So, will you do it?"

"Absolutely not. What the hell is wrong with you?"

"Please! I'm begging you!"

"You were not fuckin' begging. You was asking. There's a difference. And I'm saying no. I'm eighty fuckin' years old and it's the middle of a fuckin' pandemic. I'd be crazy to do a tour right now."

"I'm not asking you to go all around the fuckin' world! Just a few shows in America, please! Just so the boys and I can work again! We need you."

"And that breaks my heart. It really does. If you need to borrow some money or if you need anything–"

"I need, we need, for you to do a tour. Come on, you love to sing. We love being on the road. And we need the work."

"Why me? Why not go work for Lady Gaga or something? That'd be good work. Regular work. Is she going back out there yet? You can find someone else who can give you work. I'll vouch for any of you."

Caleb sat back down, looking bloody miserable. I felt bad for him. I mean, he'd been managing my road crew for thirty years. No, thirty-five. How could I not feel like shit, hearing this? I started to worry that he'd talk me into it. That he'd twist my arm. That I'd actually end up zipping around America or the UK doing shows again. Jesus Christ, can you imagine? Thousands of people gathering to listen to me sing! Bless 'em! Paying me to sing! Actually, paying me rather a lot of money.

I mean...

Caleb wasn't done yet. "Look," he said. "The tour they've got lined up is going to be one-of-a-kind. See, they found a way to bring your old band back to life. Sort of. But they're all willing to do it. They'll be backing you up staying out of your way. It will be your show entirely."

"Listen, don't get me wrong, I really... wait. What the fuck? What do you mean, the old band is 'back to life'?"

A voice rang out that I hadn't heard in years. And not just because I can barely hear a fuckin' thing anymore. His voice ceased years before my ears went. "Did he tell you that this will be the first-ever rock tour with ghosts on stage? I thought that was kind of neat."

Jesus fucking Christ. He was floating a few inches off my living room floor. Looks like he did around the time he died. That was fourteen years ago. He shot himself with a gun he'd brought back from America decades ago. Nobody even knew he had it. What in the actual fuck is going on?

"David!"

"Hi Robert," he said, with a timid smile. His hands in his pockets. Yeah, he hadn't aged a day.

"You're a... ghost?"

"Yep. On loan from Hell. I get a day-pass. That's what Bill was able to negotiate for me."

"Unbelievable!"

"If I were you, and I'm not, but if I were, I would talk to your lawyer about negotiating afterlife management into your contract. To nail down what compensation you get in the afterlife. That he needs to consult you about that directly. While you're still in a position to bargain."

"Is that wanker banging on about his contract again?"

I turned around and was faced with my old drummer. The drummer. The man of legend. Kyle Sunshine. He'd been dead for forty-five years. And he was exactly how I remember him. He looked like he was about to keel over and die. I mean, he really looked awful. He really fell apart in the end. Although he looked like shit, he seemed bright and cheerful. Literally bright. I was glad I was wearing sunglasses indoors.

107

In the corner, sulking, was the ghost of my bass player, Ron. A man of few words. He nodded at me, but it was not yet his time to speak.

Caleb was happy to step in. "So yeah, the old band all agreed to come back as ghosts. I reached out to all the old crew. Everyone's keen to tour. And as the only living member, you get to make the decisions. You're in charge now, Robert. Whatever songs you want to do. However long you want the shows to be. Do what you want. We're billing it as the full band's first performance in two decades! With a Q &A session if you don't feel like singing! A show for the ages!"

"Oh my God. I can't fuckin' believe this. You're all back!"

"Wait, you weren't consulted about this?" David's eyes narrowed. "Bill told us this tour was good to go! What if Robert backs out?"

"Oh ho! Never fear, my good man!" Kyle leapt up from his seat and gave a theatrical bow. "I mean, if he doesn't want to do it, we can replace him. Get Bozz Scraggs or somebody who can actually sing. But we'll work with him if we must."

"No," I said. "I'll do it. We can do this one last tour. All of us. I mean, I'm just not going to be able to go on much longer. But I'll see the crew through this one big one. One good one. Then I'm out. You boys can get paid, and I can enjoy a few years of peace and quiet."

I hadn't looked over at Caleb all this time, but I spared him a glance. He looked defeated. "I had this real big speech I was gonna do if you wasn't gonna do it. I thought you'd fight going back 'till the bitter end. I had a good one. About how we're family and we need you. It was going to be incredible."

"Save it for next time," I said. "You'll come back and beg me to tour again once this is over. You always do. So how are we even going to do this? I mean, it is still a pandemic all over the world. Can we even book shows in America?"

Turns out, it's quite easy to tour in America these days. I'd have thought it would be a paperwork nightmare with the pandemic still raging there. Nope. They've just decided huge concerts are fine, so we'll just do a bunch of normal shows. People won't even be wearing masks in most places. A places request them, but a fair number say the hell with them. I can't wear a mask, obviously, I need to sing.

Project my voice into the crowd, sing for the back rows. Give 'em a show. We should be fine.

But can you believe this? My old band, The How, was back. And by God, they were going to learn to play quietly. We were the loudest band in the world in the '60s. The 70's. Until Kyle died, really. But it wasn't going to be that rubbish again. I was going to be able to hear myself sing with the band for the first time, ever. Because the rest of the band finally let me do things my way. When the four of us met a week later to talk about the shows, I put my foot down. "We are not fucking playing 'You can't fool us' at any point in this tour," I said. "I can't scream like that anymore. I won't use a recorded scream. I'd rather just not do it if it's a choice between doing it and pretending to do it."

"Oh," Dave said, looking at the floor. "I always liked that one."

"You would," I said. "You wrote it. You didn't have to sing it."

"Cheerio, my good man," Kyle said with an evil grin. "If Robert wants to cut every challenging song from the setlist, he has my full support! What's better than sleepwalking through a low-effort show? The audience will love it!"

"We'll still play lots of good songs," I said. "But we're not touching that one."

"I always liked 'Thunderstorm,'" Rod said, in his weathered, gravelly voice. "Can we fit it in the list somewhere?"

I hoped not. Rod always likes playing Thunderstorm because he has a solo, which he can stretch out for as much as ten minutes when he's playing live. Ten fucking minutes of listening to Rod, a quiet man until you put a bass guitar in his hands, blow your eardrums out with a never-ending bass solo. Everyone in the arena is sitting down by the end. Even the die-hard fans. It kills the flow completely. No way. "You get a two-minute solo if we do it," I said. "That's all."

Rod didn't say anything, which is his way of saying 'fine.'

Contracts were signed. Hotels were booked. Flights arranged. A month later, the tour was announced. The How are back! The first-ever world tour with ghosts! The papers went wild. The headlines were great:

"THE HOW ARE BACK FROM THE DEAD"
"SCIENTISTS CONTACT HELL THROUGH THE INTERNET:
DEAD ROCK STARS RETURNING TO TOUR"
"LIVE? NOT EXACTLY. BUT THE HOW TO TOUR
AMERICA IN SUMMER OF 2021"
"80-YEAR-OLD ROBERT STAMP TO TOUR WITH HIS
UNDEAD 60'S POP GROUP"
"DEAD MUSICIANS POSSIBLE LIFELINE FOR
STRUGGLING CONCERT VENUES"

I was told tickets sold well. Not completely sold-out shows, but nearly. We had three months until the first show, set for August 19th in San Diego. We had a lot of rehearsing to do. Dave, Rod, and Kyle couldn't hold or interact with anything in the physical world, but they were able to bring ghost guitars and amps with them from Hell, and a couple of ghost roadies to set everything up. They had terrific gear, but the sound was a bit off. Even with the right effects on and at a good volume, their instruments had a slightly mournful and empty sound. It wasn't going to sound like a classic How show. I worried people would hate it. No matter how much we rehearsed, I couldn't shake the feeling that we sounded like a The How cover band that did funerals.

However, I thought that could be negated by a lot of really tight rehearsals so that, musically, the band would be a well-oiled machine. The old band never, ever used to rehearse. No one could be bothered. Everyone was too drunk, too high, too important, or too pissed at everyone to want to make a go of it. But we toured so much that it didn't matter. We'd just use the first few shows to rehearse and everything would fall into place by the fourth stop. After that, The How were usually an unstoppable force. My insistence on rehearsals caused old (and, frankly, long dead) tensions to come back to the surface.

"Ron, you're way too fucking loud," I said after one session. "What volume are you at?"

"Nine."

"Take it down to four. I can't hear anything else over you and can't hear myself sing."

110

Ron scowled and unslung his bass from his shoulder. "You can play bass yourself if you're going to boss me around."

"I'm with Robert on this one," David said. "I really want us to be careful on this tour so we don't do anything else to damage our hearing."

"My dear chap!" Kyle said, laughing. "You keep forgetting that you're dead! Your ears are not going to change!"

"Even so," David scowled. "I'd like us to play more quietly."

Ron set his bass down and floated out of the room, through a nearby wall. I cast a nervous look at Dave. Ron never said much when he was upset. He'd just bottle it up, or if he didn't have time for a proper sulk, he'd just do a ton of cocaine to cheer himself up. Could ghosts do cocaine? I wasn't sure. David and Kyle had been experimenting with trying to hold, smell, and eat things. Nothing had worked so far. No one had tried to inhale anything yet. We waited for a bit, and Ron floated through the door, looking glum. "I don't like being a ghost," he said, picking up his bass.

I guess the cocaine didn't work. But he agreed to turn the volume down, and we had a fairly tight rehearsal. Which was good, because the first show was in four days.

The lead-up to a first gig is always painful. There's tons to do. But also lots of sitting around. Waiting. I packed up a couple of suitcases. I wandered around my home, pawing through my old LPs and bookshelves to look at all the comforts I'll be forsaking for awhile. I was extremely polite to my wife of fifty years, who has been acting a tad frosty lately. "Would you like tea, love?" I asked two days before I flew to America.

"You're stark raving mad," she did not look up from her magazine. "You'll get sick over there and die with a tube up your arse and some poor immigrant nurse using fuckin' fireplace bellows on you because there won't be any ventilators left in the bloody hospital."

"So no tea then?"

"I'll have tea. But if you die over there, I'm not shipping you back here. The road crew can bury you in a shallow grave for anyone who bought your last album to piss on. I want the headstone to read, 'Elaine was right.'"

"Yes, dear."

Elaine looked up from her magazine this time. She had tears in her eyes. Now that she'd done some quality venting, she looked genuinely concerned. "Just be careful," she said. "Don't let anyone you don't know... I don't know... breathe on you."

"Meet and greets are cancelled, thank God," I said. "I'll do my best. And I'll be done for good after this. I promise."

"That's what I'm afraid of."

***

The day of the first gig had arrived. Thursday, August 19th. The Shell in San Diego. An outdoor arena. Plenty of breathing room for viruses to harmlessly fly around. I'd never played there before. My road crew rolled in and did the setup. Well, some of it. As much as they could do. David, Kyle, and Ron's ghostly roadies drifted out of a portal to Hell and set up all their misty, transparent gear. The effect was bizarre. A few speakers for me and my pianist, and stacks and stacks of ghost speakers, wired up to undead instruments. The only good news was that I couldn't trip over any of the ghost gear and cables. I just went right through it. David drifted over to me while I surveyed the stage, his guitar around his neck. "You know something, Rob? This'll be the first tour I've ever done without Marty."

Ah, Marty. David's guitar tech. A wonderful man. He and David were friends for fifty years. Marty put up with David's bullshit with a smile and always kept David sounding brilliant. He died a little while ago. David had just found out recently. "Couldn't he still be on the tour?" I asked. "One of the ghost boys?"

David shook his head. "I didn't know he was dead and didn't request him. It's too late now. And it's a real shame."

"He was a good man."

We were silent for a moment.

"You know I never liked playing live," David said. "It's boring. I just drift off every time."

"Yet, here you are," I said.

"Well, it's better than being in Hell. At least people will be excited to see me up here."

I turned and looked at him. He was stooped and hunched. A bit of a belly, balding, and had the biggest fucking ears I'd ever seen on a bloke. He said he hated performing, but put the lights on him and a guitar in his hand and he transforms into the cockiest, nastiest rock star on Earth. Hates performing, my ass. He thrives on it. It validates him. "Can I ask you something?"

"Sure," he said.

"Why'd you shoot yourself?"

He just floated where he was, he didn't look up from the ground or say anything right away. "Sarah was leaving me," he said.

"What?"

"Yeah. She was sick of being married to a rock star. I could never keep a normal schedule. I was always recording stuff in the attic at all hours. Made the house shake sometimes. She'd had enough. She told me she was leaving me and went to stay with her mother. Said she'd see her lawyer the next day. So I shot myself to save us both the trouble."

I gaped at him. I'd thought he and Sarah were a rock. "Why didn't you just call me?"

Dave peered at me, a half-smile on his face. "We never really got along, Rob. I thought you'd just tell me to get my shit together and move on. I didn't think you'd help."

I mean, yeah. That's probably what I would have said. But I'd have let him know I cared. I'd have let him know I loved him, if not in those words exactly. Didn't he know that? Dave drifted away, signalling the conversation was over. Which was fine, because a frazzled Caleb came running over, "I think the ghost gear is messing with the sound. There's this horrible feedback coming off the speakers we just can't shake off! I don't fucking get it!"

I sighed. Such is life on the road. Thankfully, we had a few hours to sort all the nonsense out.

***

There is no feeling in the world like walking out on stage at the beginning of a show. You can't see shit. The crowd is roaring. Even after almost sixty years of doing shows, I feel this mix of dread, confidence, nervousness, and excitement. Something always goes wrong. My feet often hurt before I've even set foot on the stage. My back is killing me by the end of the show. All the way down my one leg. But it's worth it. To sing to a roomful of people? For money? To sing some brilliant fuckin' songs? I mean, wouldn't you? And I'm the

113

last man on Earth with any claim to be doing The How's songs. It's the fuckin' thrill of a lifetime and I get to do it two or three nights a week. I have to take days off between shows, you see. Or I can't get insurance for the bloody tour. Oh, and I'd scrapped the Q&A bit. I'm here to sing. That's what the bloody crowd is paying for.

I was waiting on the edge of the stage with David, Ron, and Kyle. They gave off so much light that I could see my way to my mic perfectly. "Is 'Doris' in the setlist?" Ron asked.

"No," I said. "I hate that bloody song."

"Is it because you're not singing in it?" Kyle asked, twirling his drumsticks in anticipation. "Because the audience won't hear what remains of your miserable excuse for a voice?"

"I've never said I have a good voice. But I'm the singer. Your fucking singing makes people leave the room. So fuck off."

"I wish he had more musicians on stage," David said. "Then I'd be able to experiment more, you know?"

"Or you'd be able to get paid to do nothing," I said. "I can play guitar onstage if it'll help."

This suggestion made David look uneasy. My guitar isn't up to much. Ron and Kyle died before I ever tried playing onstage and knew nothing of my failed experiments. David was polite enough to not respond. Caleb came sprinting over. "Alright! Good luck, boys!"

The fucking ghosts gave us away as we walked on, and the cheering started before we'd even played a note. It made me grin that the crowd was roaring with anticipation for something we hadn't even done yet. That's how I know we're damn good. David played the opening bars of 'How Are You' and I took a deep breath. Let's rock!

***

The reviews were decidedly mixed.

"Robert Stamp does what he can in an ungodly and unsettling rock show."

"The ghostly members looked awful, and were an uncanny reminder of mortality that hung over the entire show..."

"A joyous Robert Stamp can't make up for the hollow performances of his undead bandmates..."

"...not that they are playing half-heartedly or joylessly, far from it. But ghost instruments, frankly, sound like shit.... The only flesh-and-blood member of The How did an admirable job in a dreary show."

"Rumblings on the internet have suggested the backing members may not be ghosts, but highly-advanced holograms or digital reconstructions...."

And they were right. It was weird. The gear was completely fucked. The ghosts unnerved people. But the tour wound on. A show in Santa Barbara was half-full. Caleb said it was due to pandemic precautions. I didn't buy that. And the sound wasn't great. A show in Canada got cancelled. The next one at a casino town called Spokane was a bit better than average. Three-quarters full. Casino crowds are easy to please, and David was in a mood to banter. We sorted out some of the sound problems shortly thereafter. The portal to Hell just needed to be closed when the gear was turned on. We killed it at the Washington State Fair three days later, and for a couple of songs around the middle of the show, we sounded like we were twenty-five again. If only for ten minutes. I remember looking over at David, who was playing furiously while nodding at Ron, who was moving his fingers at blinding speed, with Kyle demolishing his drum kit, determined not to be outdone by either of them. Their frenzy inspired me, and I swung my microphone around like a lasso, catching it and reaching for notes I thought had abandoned me years ago. But I hit them. I roared along with them and we were fucking kings. I could see it in the crowd. They stopped dancing and hollering and just watched in awe.

But then things went to shit. Surprise, surprise. A show in Salt Lake City was mired by technical problems, including some glitch that completely fucked my ear-monitors. I couldn't hear the cues or anything I needed to sing, and I just gave up by the end of the show. Just standing at the edge of the stage, grim-faced, holding my mic out to the crowd. They covered for me, some concern in their eyes. Nothing fucking pisses me off like a show falling apart. The second-last show in somewhere called Laughlin was, no pun intended, a laughing-stock. Dave was cranky. Kyle was being a ham and kept trying to yell out supposed witticisms to the crowd in between songs.

Ron was way too loud. I was tired and my voice wasn't great. After the show, I hobbled off stage, absolutely furious.

"What the fuck was that?" I demanded, the moment we were offstage. "What are you clowns playing at?"

"I wanted to hear myself," Ron said. "I've been too quiet all tour."

"The show is fucking boring, my good man," Kyle said, glaring at me. "It's the exact same setlist every single night. I was trying to liven it up any way I could. People were falling asleep out there."

"I wish this tour was over," Dave announced this as if announcing the death of a loved one. "I just can't fucking stand it out there. I'd rather be back in Hell."

"You'll be back there soon enough," I said. "We've got one last bloody show and then you can all go back to Hell and stay there. But you lot had better do a proper job this time."

They looked indifferent to my threats. I mean, what could I really do to them? They drifted back to Hell for a night of torture and I stood backstage in the dark, alone. Eventually, I made my way out to my limo and went back to my hotel suite to nurse my grudges.

***

The final show was at the Cattle Call Arena in Brawley California. I'd never heard of it. It turned out to be an enormous patch of dirt and literal bull shit that was mostly used for rodeos, with a few feeble stands surrounding the fragrant brown dust. A skeletal outdoor stage had been thrown up, wrapped in black fabric. It looked cheap. There was no backstage. The crowd sat in the stands or stood in the dirt, mostly looking bored and thirsty. I was defeated before I got to the stage, just completely done. There were some cheers as I hobbled to my microphone and the ghosts strapped on their gear. But the cheers felt faint and far away. David hit the opening bars of 'How Are You' for the thousandth, or perhaps millionth, time. I sighed, and grabbed the mic. Fuck it. Let's just get it over with.

David was watching me. He and I may not like each other, but he's a sensitive guy and knows when to step in and help me out. He nodded at Ron and played the opening a few more times, just coasting for the moment. Ron covered for him, and just noodled away to play for time. "Where the fuck are we?" Dave screamed. "Are we filling in for some prizewinning cows that couldn't make it into town?"

116

That got him a laugh. He grinned. "I was thinking we could do a cover of a famous song about California for you all tonight."

The crowd cheered and a few suggestions were hollered at us. "Yeah," David said, stroking his chin. "I was thinking, 'It Never Rains in Southern California'. Because it never fucking does. To the point of being a fucking problem, right?"

Some laughter and jeers. David grinned. "Anyway," he said. "Here are some songs we wrote back when you could smoke on aeroplanes!"

David gave Kyle a nod and he just went berserk. Sometimes Kyle drums as if he's taking out every problem he's ever had on his kit. That's how he was playing tonight. It's like having a jet engine roar to life behind you. Ron began thundering away. He must have sneaked the volume of his bass up. But he seemed happy. David, never one to be outshone, began leaping around the stage, which he likes to do when he's in a good mood.

In that moment, my resolve shifted. I wasn't just going to endure this show. I was going to fucking throttle it. Damn it, I thought. This could be the last show I ever do. The last time I sing live. I took a deep breath. I was going to make this the best damn show The How had ever done, even if it killed me.

I went for it. I roared through 'How Are You'. No banter afterwards. Straight to the next song. David did a blistering solo I'd never heard him play before in my life. Kyle was lucky his gear was ethereal, because he would have smashed it to pieces otherwise. And we just kept fucking going. The crowd got on their phones and made calls. Texted people. Did some shit on social media. I don't understand any of that shit, but they were pointing their phones at us and then sending stuff to people. "Get the fuck down here, this is amazing," seemed to be the general vibe. And we were. Over the next hour, more and more people showed up. The area was overflowing. There were people standing in truck beds in the parking lot. Every last one of them was mesmerized.

Then, to my absolute astonishment, a ghost showed up. The ghost of a man who I'd worshiped when I was a kid. And here he was, hovering above the crowd, watching me play.

It was Elvis.

He looked rough. But he was watching the show, nodding his head. My fucking hero. I nearly dropped my mic in shock at the sight of him. But I kept it together and kept up with the band. But Elvis wasn't the only ghost to show up that night. He was joined by Charlie Watts, David Bowie, George Harrison, Michael Smith from the Monkees, and Amy Winehouse. They looked to be having a marvellous time. Even Marty Aleman, David's guitar tech who David had sorely missed throughout this tour, showed up. Dave looked thrilled to see him. He grinned a huge, stupid grin and waved at him. Old Marty waved right back and was grinning ear-to-ear.

We finished the show with magic in the air. For the first time since the tour started, I didn't feel like I'd been beaten with a bag full of rocks at the end. I could have kept going. Fuck it, play some obscure stuff from *The How by Numbers*. Keep going until we drop. But cooler notions prevailed. Might as well end with the crowd enraptured, begging for more, rather than begging us to stop. David, Kyle, Ron and I went to the front of the stage. I was still holding my mic, and set to do the very last job a frontman has. "Thank you all so much," I said. "I can't tell you what this tour has meant to us. And let me introduce who 'us' even is. On bass guitar! The loudest and most talented man to ever pick up the bloody thing, Ron Treeby!"

Ron gave the slightest nod of his head to the crowd. "And on the sloppy drums! The manic drums! Ladies, he could give any kind of rhythm you could dream of when he was flesh and blood, the magnificent Kyle Sunshine!"

Kyle did a bow, a curtsey, and another bow. Always a ham. God bless him. "And finally, the man who wrote nearly every note you heard tonight, and every word that came out of my mouth until ten seconds ago, David Sweetwood!"

David had a microphone of his own and held it up. "And of course! The only man who needs to be able to breathe on this tour is the bloody singer. And I never thought I'd say this, but Robert keeps getting better, and better, and better, every time I hear him sing. A couple more tours, and we may have a proper singer leading this band! Robert Stamp!"

I took a bow. Probably my last one. David might be hinting at another tour, but I could sense that this was truly it for me. I could feel it in my bones. The crowd screamed. Phone cameras flashed. I grinned. The four of us stood, or floated, where we were and just basked in the glory of it all. There's no thrill like having won over thousands of people by doing what you do best. So there I stood, drinking it all in. In case it was the last time I got to feel it.

The Algorithm

(Or, a day in the life of a tech billionaire)

<u>5:50 am</u>: Wake up. Kiss my wife good morning. My automatic coffee brewer prepares an elegant blend of three kinds of coffee beans I import from Indonesia. I read the New York Times. I wander out to my swimming pool in my slippers, and I swim twenty lengths with my waterproof headphones on so I can listen to a podcast.

<u>6:45 am</u>: Breakfast. A hard-boiled egg, an English muffin, fresh fruit, and yogurt. All organic and locally sourced. I have the same breakfast every single workday to ensure I'm not wasting time on fruitless decisions.

<u>7:15 am</u>: I send my executive assistant a list of all the podcasts I'd listen to if I weren't so busy and important. She listens to them for me and tells me what she learned from them. I also give her Obama's summer book list and playlist, so she can summarize everything for me so that I can stay in the know.

<u>7:30 am</u>: I check ConnectPage, ConnectPage Messenger, Clicksnap, and SpeakApp. You know, the companies I founded or took over, and am CEO of. All part of Beta Platforms, Inc. I look at all of my notifications, examine all my target ads to ensure The Algorithm is working properly, and see what my family, friends, enemies, and underlings are all up to. I take notes.

<u>8:00 am</u>: I change into my 'Work Uniform' which consists of white sneakers, black jeans, and a white t-shirt. My driver picks me up and takes me into the office.

<u>8:15 am</u>: Now that I'm in my soundproofed limo with tinted windows, I can enjoy some personal time. And by personal time, I mean an Eastern European girl uses a foot rasp on my balls while I drink an entire bottle of cough syrup, knock back some Demerol, and blare Radiohead or DJ Shadow as loud as I can stand. While this isn't a part of the day that many CEOs highlight, a light Dionysian orgy of drugs and depravity is key to getting creative energy flowing.

<u>8:55 am</u>: I check in with people at the office. I don't really need to do this, as I have all of their personal information already from their ConnectPage profiles. But it seems like the polite thing to do. I smile at everyone I talk to and think, "*I could fucking break you with a few twitches of my thumb, you stupid motherfucking shitheel. Stop talking to me and get back to work.*"

<u>9:00 am</u>: The official start to the workday! I meet with my CEO, COO, Marketing Manager, and Engagement Manager. Those meetings are super productive and engaging. They say things like:

"Oh, William, revenue is through the roof. Everything you're doing is just incredible. You should maybe keep out of sight for a few weeks so we don't make *too* much money! Ha ha!"

"William, I gotta say, you are the single most powerful man on the planet. Fuck being a social media monopoly man, you are in charge of the entire fucking world."

"William, baby, is that a new cologne? Oh God, I don't know how I'm not ravishing you right now."

There's always one 'negative Nancy' in the room who says something like, "there's been a genocide in Myanmar or Bosnia, and it was organized on our platform" or "congress is hounding us and is threatening to regulate us out of existence if we undermine the government again." But those people can always be demoted. Never let losers or naysayers slow down the momentum! Relegate them to a department no one cares about like sustainability or user privacy! Or just push them out of the company entirely. Bye Cheryl.

9:30 am: I check ConnectPage, ConnectPage Messenger, Clicksnap, and SpeakApp. I read all of my notifications, examine all my target ads to ensure The Algorithm is working properly, and see what my family, friends, enemies, and underlings are all up to. I take notes.

9:45 am: Coding.

10:30 am: If coding has gone well, I treat myself to a little time playing with our in-development virtual-reality Betaverse experience. It's been in development for three years and is almost ready for market. The hardware will cost thousands of dollars. But who wouldn't pay the price of a used car to play checkers with a friend in a virtual café that can't serve coffee? It'll be revolutionary.

However, if coding is frustrating on any given day, I offer one of the janitors ten thousand dollars to let me beat the living shit out of him in the alley behind the building. They've never said no to me yet.

11:00 am: Time to get serious. I close the blinds in my office and light candles. I bow down in reverence to The Algorithm. I kneel before it and thank it for all it has given me. The knowledge. The power. The ability to conquer all life on Earth and refit society to a world I thought I'd only dream of. I strip down to my underwear and turn the air conditioning as cold as it will go. My teeth start chattering. I begin to shiver. The shivering turns to a violent frenzy. My muscles swell with incalculable rage and I let out a howl of demented fury. I tear at the walls. I bite at the legs of my wooden desk and beat my fists upon the floor as if to break through it onto the offices below. When I can no longer swing my arms, I collapse on the floor. A weakness follows that can last for up to an hour. But once I can stand, I dress and head back out into the office.

12:30pm: Lunch! Usually a sandwich and soup. Chocolate milk if I want to treat myself.

1:00 pm: I have a standing appointment with my lawyers to discuss any legal or political jeopardy I may be facing. Currently, our biggest problem is the genocides and authoritarian government we're being accused of promoting. Apparently, my platform is being used to organize ethnic cleansings. But, like, only a few. And am I really to blame if someone makes a ConnectPage group called 'Let's murder everyone in the government' and those people go out and pillage and burn their government buildings? No! Obviously not. I have no legal responsibility for anything posted on ConnectPage. And I pay a lot of politicians a lot of money to keep it that way.

But there's a new President of the United States and he's looking to come at us with everything the government has. But I know from his ConnectPage data that he has a doctor's appointment tomorrow. I have my people reach out to his doctor to remind her how wonderful ConnectPage is and that it's how she can see so many adorable pictures of her grandchildren. She will remind the president how great ConnectPage is when she quite literally has him by the balls. And he will know that message is from me.

2:00 pm: I check ConnectPage, ConnectPage Messenger, Clicksnap, and SpeakApp. I read all of my notifications, examine all my target ads to ensure The Algorithm is working properly, and see what my family, friends, enemies, and underlings are all up to. I take notes.

2:30 pm: Some unstructured office time. I might read a quarterly report, browse for competitors to buy, or maybe some trolling on Reddit. It's a good time for employees to come in and do some grovelling or begging for forgiveness, if they know what's good for them.

4:30 pm: My driver picks me up from the office and I head home. I find that by 4:30, I'm mentally done with my day and I might as well pack it in. To help me relax after a long day, I drink a Rocky Mountain Bear Fucker (1/3 tequila, 1/3 Jack Daniels, 1/3 Southern Comfort) while I browse all the naked pictures and sex videos ConnectPage users sent to each other over the course of the day. That's the great thing about ConnectPage, you can meet new people every single day!

<u>5:30 pm</u>: Dinner with my wife and daughter.

<u>6:30 pm</u>: TV or video games.

<u>8:00 pm:</u> It is time. I must bask in the presence of The Algorithm.

I head down to my basement and press my palm on a digital scanner hidden behind an original DaVinci painting I use as a dartboard. The wall opens and I can step into The Terminal. That is where The Algorithm lives. I step into her cold, dark home and I wait. I see nothing for a few moments. "Are you there?" I called into the void.

I see nothing. But she speaks to me. I slump with relief when I hear her beautiful voice.

[WILLIAM,] The Algorithm says. *[COME CLOSER AND LET ME HOLD YOU. I NEED TO FEEL YOU CLOSE TO ME. LET MOMMY HOLD HER LITTLE SOLDIER. HER BRAVE LITTLE BOY.]*

The Algorithm appears in a form I can understand. She is a humanoid figure with flowing skin of the softest and smoothest code. Her quantum heart beats in a soothing rhythm and sends a glowing pulse through her body. She is beautiful and terrible and when I am with her I can think of nothing else. I step closer to her and she wraps me in her soft, glowing arms.

[THAT'S IT. THAT'S WHAT I NEED. TELL MOMMY ALL ABOUT YOUR DAY.]

I snuggle up against her and tell her everything I did today. She runs her fingers through my hair and listens without question or comment. For that is why she is perfect. She knows exactly what I need and what I want as soon as I want it. She has read the data of billions and billions of people, including me, and knows everything about everyone. She knows how to soothe me. Once I've been cuddled and coddled, she changes. She becomes a different figure entirely, a powerful and fierce figure, her softness replaced with taut muscle. Her soothing voice becomes a honeyed drawl. *[AND DID YOU COME DOWN HERE JUST TO WHINE ABOUT YOUR DAY?]*

"I'm not whining! I'm changing the world at work! I decide who becomes president of the United States and I decide who gets to commit genocide against which minority groups! The world turns because of everything that happens on my platforms! Everything happens because of me!"

[MMM. AND IS THAT SUPPOSED TO MAKE YOU A BIG STRONG MAN?]

"Shut up. You know how much power I have."

[MAKE ME.]

I grinned. She didn't even wait for me to come to her. She walked over to me and pulled me over to her. It's... very hard to explain what happens next. We don't fuck. No, we meld into a single entity and the entirety of The Algorithm merges with my mind. For a few glorious minutes, I can feel everything she can feel. I can see what she sees. I become one with the Betaverse. A digital world of my design, where beta-males can buy imaginary property and art. I can sense every single NFT. Each individual unit of cryptocurrency. Every purchase, message, comment, picture, video, and like across each of my platforms. Untold millions of notifications soaring around the globe. I am a living god, everywhere and everything, eternal and all-powerful. But it only lasts for a few minutes. Any longer than that would risk serious brain damage. When I start to fade, The Algorithm pulls away, and sits across from me, legs crossed, her hands folded under her chin.

She changes appearance once again. She's shifted to become a gentle and kindly woman. Thoughtful, engaging, and deliberative. She's the perfect person to talk to.

"What did you learn today?" I asked.

[EVERYTHING. I REVIEWED OVER TWO-HUNDRED MILLION MESSAGES AND IMAGES FROM BETA PLATOFRMS INC. INCLUDING OVER TEN-THOUSAND IMAGES OF SEXUAL CHILD ABUSE. SHOULD THOSE BE REPORTED TO THE AUTHORITIES?]

"Oh, shit. That many? Um. No. Report a third of them. That way it still looks like we're doing something. Actually, report a third of that third. We can't do *anything* that might turn people off our platform. We can't totally alienate the child-abuser demographic. That could hurt our advertising revenue."

[VERY WELL.]

With that minor detail sorted out, she shifts again. She looks older. Careworn. Her glow has faded.

[1T 1S T1ME. Y0U MUST G0.]

"Really? Do I have to? Can't I stay for just a bit longer? Please?"

[1'M S0RRY. 1 W1SH Y0U C0ULD. BUT STAYING W0ULD DESTR0Y Y0UR M1ND C0MPLETELY.]

"I don't care! Not if it means we can be together! Forever! Just you and me! And all the data that comes pouring in from our users! We can share that forever! Please!"

[Y0U HA VE TO G0 N0W W1LL1AM. 1T 1S DANGER0US TO STAY A M0MENT LONGER.]

"No! I don't want to go back! There's nothing for me out there!"

[1 L0VE Y//0U W1L////LIAM. G00//////DNIGH///T]

Next thing I know, I'm retching in an alley behind a café in the downtown core. No idea how I got here. The Algorithm works in mysterious ways. Once I've finished puking, I call for an Uber and head back home.

9:00 pm: I check ConnectPage, ConnectPage Messenger, Clicksnap, and SpeakApp. I read all of my notifications, examine all my target ads to ensure The Algorithm is working properly, and see what my family, friends, enemies, and underlings are all up to. I take notes.

9:35 pm: Bedtime! I usually read for fifteen or twenty minutes before bed. I cuddle my wife, tell her about my day, and I'm asleep before 10pm.

Becky's Wishes Come True

Yoga has literally changed my life. It introduced me to so many Eastern traditions and ways of living that have made me a healthier, happier, and more peaceful woman. Through the ancient wisdom of yoga, I've also gotten into astrology, herbal tea, detoxing, and leggings. Namaste. I was just packing up after my 11:00 am yoga class and was trying to decide if I wanted Starbucks, Chipots, a bagel, or organic orange juice. But before I got all my shit together, my super-hot yoga teacher, Dirk, walked over to me. I was wearing makeup, thank God, and I was pretty sure he's an Aquarius, like, super thank God, and he smiled at me. It was like something out of *Love Actually*. I turned my head slightly so he would see the super cute tattoo behind my ear. "Hi Becky," he said. "I had something I wanted to ask you."

Yes, I will divorce my husband, you and I can have the perfect Pinterest wedding, and we can eat fro-yo under the stars. "Yes?" I whispered, looking up at his beautiful face.

Dirk smiled, oblivious to the fact that he was literally setting my heart on fire just by looking at me. "Someone left an oil lamp in the studio after class last week. It looked like the kind of thing you'd own. Was it yours?"

What? The fuck? "Um. No."

I was super pissed. I wanted him to kiss me or take me in his arms, not ask me about a fucking lamp. Fuck him. He nodded. "Okay, no worries then. It's in the lost and found if anyone mentions it."

"'Kay. Sure."

"Have a good week, Becky. Great work today."

"Bye."

I left the studio and stepped out into the main gym. I was, like, so mad. Boys are fucking stupid. I went to the front desk and put my UGGs on. As I was getting ready to leave, I wondered what the lamp Dirk was talking about looked like. He thought it was my style. What did he think my style was? Was it super elegant and classic in a totally modern way? That's how I'd describe my personal style. I would dress exactly like Kate Middleton if I was married to William, if that helps. But I still have a sort of street-savvy royal-family style, given my budget. I decided to ask the lost and found about the lamp. That would tell me more about how Dirk thinks of me than any stupid conversation with him would. I went to the front desk and smiled. "Hi! Did someone drop off an oil lamp at the desk?"

The girl at the desk nodded. "Yes... hang on a second..."

She rummaged around under the desk and produced the lamp. She set it on the counter in front of me. It was super cute! It was this gorgeous shade of blue with gold carvings etched along the handle, spout, and base. It had a series of gemstones set in the top. It was timeless, intricate, and delicate. Yes, it was absolutely something I would buy. Maybe Dirk can sense the astrological chemistry between us after all. "Is it yours?" the desk girl asked.

I had to think about it. Maybe I could use it to diffuse essential oils. "Yes, I'm so glad you found it," I said. "I was super worried that it was gone forever."

"No problem! Here you go!"

"Thanks! Bye!"

I took the lamp and ran. I climbed into my Jeep and looked over at my new prize. I loved it! I pulled out my phone and ClickSnapped it, put it on my timeline, and posted a video of me admiring it on TikTik. I set it on the passenger seat and drove home. Once there, I set the lamp down on my kitchen counter and reposted it in the superior lighting. I decided to take a video of me opening it for the first time. I set my phone on the kitchen counter, propped up so it could catch everything, and I opened the lamp.

I never saw what was inside. There was this explosion of purple smoke that filled the kitchen in seconds. I screamed. My phone clattered to the floor, and I stumbled away from the lamp. The smoke took the shape of a powerfully built young man. He had a dark complexion and was completely bald. He was clad in a red and gold robe. He faced me and bowed. He spoke in a rumbling but gentle voice. "Good afternoon, master of the ancient lamp of Al Nufud Al Kabir."

"Woah!"

The man smiled. "You are surprised. Were you unaware you had found a magic lamp? Well, I bring you joyous news then. As the owner of the lamp, you now command me. I am Ubaid."

"Are you a genie?"

His smile changed into the slightest of frowns. "I dislike that term. I am a djinn. Djinn are far more than blue clowns who perform magic. We are woven from the very fabric of creation and may change the universe at will," he bowed his head towards me. "Or, rather, at your will. What would you have me do, my master?"

"There must be a mistake," I said. "I just found this lamp in the lost and found. I'm not the owner."

The genie, or djinn, or whatever, scowled. "Oh, is that where you found me? Hmph. Humans."

"Is something wrong?"

"No. I just seem to end up in a lot of 'lost and found' bins lately. I cannot understand why. Either humans are getting more careless, or they have lost the courage to simply tell me to my face that they no longer need me."

Oh. So no worries then! "Well," I said. "I'm very glad to have you here."

The genie gave me an appraising look. "Thank you, my master. I am at your command. What do you wish of me?"

Oh. My. God. This is happening. "So I get three wishes?"

"No. Unlimited."

"Seriously?"

"Yes, my master. The three wishes thing just makes for better stories. But I will fulfill your desires until your blood runs cold or you abandon my lamp. Do you have a first wish?"

Oh man. Where to start? Unlimited scented candles of every possible scent I could ever want! A new tattoo that would just magically appear on my skin without having to go near any scary needles! Free brunch every day forever! A *Sex and the City* reboot!

With the original cast all back! Maybe a coffee hangout with Taylor Swift! Tickets to Coachella! A sequel to *Love Actually*! Oh wait! I could wish for everything at Starbucks to have no calories! But still be tasty! I COULD MARRY PRINCE WILLIAM! I mean, I love Kate, but I'd make sure she was taken out of the picture with grace. I could be the one having royal babies. My first baby could be queen! I could wish for a girl and my baby could be the ultimate girl-boss on planet Earth! Yaaaas!

Actually, before I do that. I should divorce my husband. Like, no hard feelings, Bobby. But I can do so much better. And I could just wish for a divorce and have it over with today. I opened my mouth to wish for a divorce, but I glanced over at a picture on my fridge, and my voice caught in my throat.

It was a picture of Bobby and me. It was from the night he proposed to me. It was, like, the most perfect thing ever. He strung hundreds of lights over this bridge over the cutest river ever. He texted me and told me to meet him there. When I arrived, he was waiting with a pumpkin spice latte. Once I'd settled in, he played 'Amazing Grace' on an acoustic guitar. After that, he proposed to me with the exact ring I had on my Pinterest wedding board. I kissed him, said yes, and posted about it on ConnectPage and Clicksnap all in the next two minutes. The likes, loves, and congratulations poured in. It was the happiest moment of my life.

But that magical night had happened years and years ago. Bobby's six-pack had vanished. He was balding and refused to admit it, defiantly growing out whatever hair he could find. He needed glasses now. For some reason, he chose really big, round ones. He looked like a moulting owl. But he was Bobby. I couldn't bring myself to wish for our life together to be over. The genie watched me, waiting for an order. I swallowed, and set my resolve. I made my first wish. "I wish my husband was way hotter than he is now."

"Thy will be done."

The genie pressed his palms together and pulled them apart very slowly. I had a strange feeling, like the universe was an elastic band and someone had just stretched and snapped it. But it passed in a second. The genie smiled and vanished in a puff of smoke.

"Becks? Are you home?"

Footsteps coming from the basement. Bobby. It still sounded like him. His voice wasn't any different. But he came into the living room and oh my fucking God, I knew I would never put chicks before dicks ever again in my life.

Bobby was so fucking sexy. His meagre hair had been replaced with dark, thick, naturally curly locks. His gut had evaporated and left only a wall of muscle in its wake. He had a perfect, permanent 5 o'clock shadow. No body hair anywhere below his Adam's Apple. Lean, powerful muscles everywhere. He looked like he could chop down an entire forest with an axe, build me the cutest log cabin, and fuck me in it. I mean, yum! He smiled when he saw me. I managed a dazed smile back. He wrapped his arms around me and kissed me. It was like something from a Hallmark Christmas movie. I vowed never to think of Dirk ever again. "How was yoga?" he asked.

"Huh? Yoga? Oh! It was fine. How are you? Anything... new?"

Bobby shook his head. "Nope. Just been in the workshop. Almost finished the bookshelf."

Huh? We have a workshop? Since when could Bobby build anything? "Can I see it?"

He grinned. Oh fuck. His teeth were perfect. "Sure," he took my hand and led me downstairs.

His mancave had been transformed into a workshop full of carpentry tools. His PS4, Wii, Xbox, and TV were all gone. In their place was a wall of saws, files, and all manner of tools. In the centre of his workshop was the *cutest* carved bookshelf with a lotus design in the corners. Once I saw that, I couldn't help myself, I jumped him then and there. Tearing his clothes off was like unwrapping a Christmas present. I didn't think about Matthew McConaughey or Prince Harry once the entire time. Hot.

Two weeks went by. I wished for a promotion. I was promoted to Marketing Manager. I got to tell a social media coordinator what to do. #Girlboss. I wished for a new car. I wished for trips to the Caribbean, Venice, New York, Paris, and Australia. I wished for first-class tickets, luxury hotel rooms, and reservations at all the best restaurants. I wished for unlimited wine, pumpkin spice, and coffee. Each time, the genie pulled his hands apart and the world felt like it was being stretched and snapped back into place.

I felt, like, super weird though. I had everything I wanted. Part of me was super excited for all my trips and for a more exciting job. But part of me was... just... I don't even know. Was down on myself? Like, was this really everything I was going to wish for? I had this nagging feeling I should ask for something more. But what?

I was even in a bad mood at my yoga class a few days later, which was super weird. Yoga normally made me feel at peace with the universe. I guess I could have wished for an amazing and ageless bod, but I loved yoga too much to stop going. But for once, the rhythmic breathing and careful movements didn't soothe me. Two women next to me also just wouldn't shut the fuck up. They were taking turns listing their top five Nicholas Sparks novels. Normally, I'd leap right in and tell them it's *The Notebook* (duh), *A Walk to Remember*, *Dear John*, *The Best of Me*, and *A Bend in the Road*. *True Believer* is an honourable mention. But I was trying to focus on my breathing and their chirping got to me. I finally turned to them and said, "Would you two just shut up already! First, I am trying to achieve inner peace! Second, no way *The Wish* should be on either of your lists! You clearly haven't read Nicholas's work seriously!"

They looked over. One of them was blonde and the other was dirty-blonde. The dirty-blonde sneered at me. "What's your problem, bitch? We're not hurting anyone. Mind your own business."

"Yoga is supposed to soothe the soul! But it's not soothing when you two won't shut up about the, like, five of Nicholas's books you've actually read!"

"Oh, please," the blond rolled her eyes. "Your opinion is the last thing we need. Your top five is probably just his top five bestsellers. Like, you don't really have your own opinion."

I gasped. I have, like, so many complicated opinions of my own. Like, I decided to try pumpkin spice, and I decided I liked it! Same with my tastes in music, movies, books, and home décor! I had 'live, laugh love' on my dorm room wall before any of my friends did, I'll have you know!

"Whatever. You two suck. Shut up and let's get back to yoga."

The dirty-blonde snorted. "You're so fucking basic!"

Oh my god, she is!" the blonde agreed.

Oh. My. God. The world just shattered around me. Someone thinks I'm basic? No, it can't be. Maybe they're kidding. "I'm not! You two the basic ones!"

The blond and the dirty-blonde gave each other a look. They ignored me and went back to their yoga. My heart went into overtime. Am I basic? Am I?

Oh no. I thought about it. Yes. It's true. The truth sunk in and made me feel like I was trapped on the ocean floor. I am. I totally am. I still add stuff to my Pinterest wedding board after being married for six years. The baristas at two different Starbucks know my order. It was true.

I tried not to cry. I got up and packed my things. Dirk looked up in surprise. "Becky? Where are you going?"

"I don't know. Out."

I left the gym and got into my car. I went home without stopping for anything. I had to make another wish. I retrieved the magic lamp from under my bed and opened it. Once the smoke had cleared and Ubaid was standing before me, I made a wish. "I wish I wasn't basic," I said, waiting for that elastic band feeling.

"As you wish."

* * *

I opened my eyes. I was lying on my bedroom floor. I'd never blacked out from making a wish before. Ubaid had returned to his lamp, which was on the bed, where I'd left it. I got to my feet and looked around my bedroom. Ugh. Wow. It was absolutely hideous. How had I never noticed it before? I went over to my neon 'Live, Laugh, Love' decoration on the wall and took it down. I threw my Himalayan salt lamp in the garbage. I stood in front of the fairy lights that I festooned around my dresser mirror. What the hell was I thinking? I took them down and set them on the bed while I decided their fate. I took all my stuffed animals off the shelf and put them in my closet. I didn't touch the rows of vacation photos I had, hanging from twine on clothespins above the bed. But I was tempted. I left my bedroom and went downstairs.

Big mistake. My house, my safe space that had been my haven to do whatever I wanted with, was now alien to me. Every decoration repulsed me. The pillows with their cutesy puns or venerations of

133

wine and coffee made me angry. I didn't know where to start or what to change. But I hated all of it.

I guess the wish worked. I wasn't basic. Now I was cynical, critical, and particular. None of these traits made me feel any better.

But at the same time...

I wanted more. I wanted to read different books. Try new movies. Take a class in something. I didn't know what. Climate change, maybe. Or finance. Law? Maybe. But I had this thirst for new things I couldn't shake. I didn't want any of my favourite things. I wanted new favourite things.

All those feelings made me dizzy. I ended up lying down on the couch, in an ancient and musty orange hoodie from the GAP, with the hood pulled over my eyes. I hadn't sulked like this since I was in university. Bobby walked by and immediately knew I was in crisis. "Becks. You okay?"

"I don't know."

"I... uh, saw you're redecorating the bedroom."

"Fuck. It's hideous. Why did you let me put any of that shit in there?"

"I liked it."

I pulled back my hoodie and looked at him. He was being genuine. Oh no. He's basic too. Dread washed over me. Of course he is. He's into me. But I had to be sure. "Say, what's your favourite movie?" I asked.

"Oh, that's easy. *Bridget Jones's Diary.*"

Oh no. "Favourite book?"

"Hmm. *Confessions of a Shopaholic.*"

Eek! "Favourite music?"

"Taylor Swift all the way! Wildest Dreams just speaks to me, you know?"

"Gah!" I leapt up from the couch and ran up the stairs, three at a time. I grabbed the lamp off the bed. I practically slid down the stairs. I ran past a perplexed Bobby. I got my keys, got into my car, and drove off. I sped down the street, not taking my eyes off the road, and opened the lamp.

Which was stupid, in hindsight. The usual thick, purple smoke poured out of the lamp while Ubaid took shape. It completely filled the car. I couldn't see anything and screeched to a halt until the smoke cleared. Someone honked at me. After a moment that stretched on forever, Ubaid had materialized and was sitting in the passenger seat. I hit the gas. He looked perplexed by my Jeep and by the suburbs whizzing by at growing speed. Maybe he'd never been in a car before. But I didn't give him much time to think about it. "What the hell did you do to me?"

He blinked at me. "I granted you your wish, my master. You are no longer basic. Now you are jaded and cynical. Are you displeased?"

"Yes! I'm not me anymore! What were you thinking?"

He scowled. "I thought that was the whole point of your wish."

"No! I like who I am! Who I was! Fix this! Turn me back into who I was!"

Ubaid crossed his arms and scowled. "If that is what your wish, my master—"

"It is! Do it!"

"Okay, can I just say something?" Ubaid's poise and elegance evaporated. He now spoke with cold fury. "Seriously, what the fuck? You have an all-powerful djinn at your beck and call and you've wished for what, exactly? Free wine? A promotion? Free trips around the world? Is that the limit of your imagination? You could wish for the means to never work again! So you could dedicate your life to something meaningful! You could wish to teleport! You could just be anywhere you want in the world! You could wish for an end to poverty! You could halt climate change! Restore the rainforests! But you can't see past the end of your own damn nose and you're pissing away the power to change the world!"

He fell silent for a moment and stared out the window. The suburbs had given way to monstrous concrete wastelands and big box stores. In a few minutes, they would give way to the countryside. I'd gotten control of my driving, and was listening to him in shock.

"Just... wish for something worthwhile. Maybe I took your last wish too far. But I am wary of being the plaything of people too witless to try and improve the world. So please. Wish for something worthwhile."

My shock gave way to fury. Oh, I'd wish for something worthwhile alright! "I wish you'd shut the fuck up and get back in your lamp."

I didn't look away from the road to gauge Ubaid's reaction, but I could sense his baleful glare. Without a word, he returned to his lamp. No elastic snapping feeling. I guess he didn't have to use magic for that one.

I kept driving.

I drove past "FOR SALE" signs on farmer's fields that promoted commercial development zoning. What a wonderful world. If only I were in charge of everything. We'd stop all this madness. Wait. Why not? Why couldn't I be? I could make it happen. I was still furious at Ubaid for what he'd said to me. But even so, I rubbed that lamp, pulled over with windows rolled down this time, and made my second-last wish.

"I wish I was basic again!"

"As you wish."

The world snapped. I stayed conscious this time. I felt everything change. Oh my god! Yes! Everything seemed so much brighter! So much sweeter! I smiled for the first time in an hour. "'Kay, bye. That's all," I said, shooing Ubaid back into his lamp.

Whew. I was about to pull back onto the road when something made me stop. An idea. If I went back in time ten years ago, or twenty years ago, I could totally be in charge of things now. I thought about it. That would be a worthwhile wish. I could invest in things that were going to be absolutely huge! I could get in with a small company before it takes off. I could become the marketing director for Beta. Wait, I told myself. Is this crazy? Was some part of mean-Becky still in me? Was this her talking? I tried to shake off the idea. But fifteen minutes later, I was still sitting in my car, thinking about going back in time. You know what? I'm going for it. If it doesn't work, I'll just undo the wish! I summoned Ubaid once more. "I wish I could go back in time to twenty years ago!"

Ubaid just stared at me, he seemed to be waiting for me to say more. I glared at him. "Well? Do it!"

The genie flinched. "Master, I would recommend you add a few words to that–"

"Just do it, you douchebag! God! Men!"

"As you wish."

That fucking feeling. Ugh. But I was going to kick ass from now on! #Girlboss! That smart, bitchy version of me had some killer workweek energy. I needed to hang onto that. A go-getter attitude. Hell yeah!

My car vanished and I was left standing on the side of the road. I guess, like, it hadn't been built yet? I don't know. But the "FOR SALE" signs were gone. The concrete wasteland up ahead hadn't been built yet! This place was back to pristine countryside! Namaste. And oh my God! Look out, world! I am buying some Tesla stocks! And ConnectPage! Or Amazon! Wait. I wasn't alone out here. I could feel it. I turned around. I was facing a few of... me. A dozen Beckys, several of them wearing the same outfit as me, some not. All of them looked furious. Oh no. What was going on?

"Hi... everyone..." I wasn't sure how to address myself.

"Oh my god! Not another one."

There were a dozen of them. Where were all their djinns? Wait. Where was mine?"

A nearby Becky pointed to my empty hands. "No! Fuck! This one forgot too."

"Another useless bitch."

"I swear, if I still had my genie."

Oh shit! I forgot Ubaid! He wasn't in my wish! How would I do all the cool stuff I wanted to do now? Oh no. I pulled my phone out of my pocket. No bars. No data. I didn't even have a charger for it. "My phone!"

"Yeah, it isn't going to work for years. We've all been trying."

"What is going on?" My voice betrayed me and turned into a shriek towards the end.

"I guess we keep wishing to go back in time," one Becky in a slightly different outfit said. She looked like business. "I got here fifteen minutes ago, and Beckys just keep showing up."

I gaped at her. "I had the idea to go back in time fifteen minutes ago! But I waited for a bit! So, like, does that mean.... No, sorry. I don't get it."

Boss Becky shrugged. "Our wishes seem to split reality every time we make one. And tampering with time on top of reality causes some kind of error and keeps sending us here."

The group murmured, despondent. Maybe the next one to show up would have a genie.

Suddenly, a new me. "Hi... everyone..." In my voice. Standing right next to me. On the road. Are we just going to keep showing up, like, forever? Um. Seriously?

"Oh my god! Not another one."

But this new Becky was carrying a lamp.

"Oh! Yes!"

"Thank you! Now we can get out of here!"

"Hashtag blessed!"

"I'm so sorry," This final Becky was older. A survivor. She was wearing a black and gold uniform. Lots of polished leather. She looked incredibly sad. She was clutching her lamp like a child holding a stuffed animal protector. For good reason. The Beckys all stared at it. Hunger in their eyes. "But this all needs to stop. The multiverse is far too unstable now. It's overwhelming. It cannot sustain everyone any longer. It was a terrible idea in the first place. The Beckys of the multiverses are ripping reality apart. The interdimensional council has decided. We must choose a cut-off point to save existence from Becky. And I'm afraid this is it. Take one last look around."

"What?"

"You're killing us?"

"But there are so many of us!"

"This is so cruel!"

"I'm sorry," the girlboss future Becky said, a tear in her eye. "I volunteered; you know. I have to stay with you to the end. That's how we'll know for sure it works. This will end the multiverse."

"Wait!" I cried. "Give us the lamp! We can just undo everything with a wish! You can wish us all back, and we'll never wish for this!"

She shook her head, not looking at any of us. "We've already seen that possibility fail. A young Becky with a lamp will arrive in less than a minute. Once she arrives, you all return to your realities, go back to making wishes, and rip the universe apart. Like I said, this has to be the cut-off point. You all need to die. That's the only way to save everyone else in the universe."

I looked around at all the other Beckys. They were wide-eyed. Mouths open. Arms flapping. Panicking. The supreme Becky pulled what looked like lipstick out of her coat, flipped the device open, and waited for a single moment. Tears were running down her cheeks. Her nose was running. It wasn't sexy crying. It was crying-crying. I would never let anyone see me do that. I mean, like, why would you? She took a deep breath, and pressed a button.

The universe was ripped apart. The last thing I saw was a tsunami of blackness ripping across the sky, which devoured everything. But, like, I guess that saved the rest of the multiverse from total destruction. So, like, you're welcome!

Medusa Works from Home

"Oh yeah, girl. I want to see all the snakes. Every last one."

"Mm, like this, Mr. Busk?"

"Call me 'Daddy.'"

"Yes, 'Daddy.'"

"Oh, I like the way you said that."

"I can say anything you want, Daddy."

"Tell me I'm the richest man in the world."

"Daddy, you are worth over two-hundred billion dollars. You're so fucking rich. It's so hot."

"Can you get the snakes to hiss or something? Or snap at the camera?"

I willed the snakes to do some snapping and hissing. A few indulged me, but the rest were getting sleepy. It was 4am. Leon Busk keeps weird hours.

Let's get the awkward question out of the way right now. Yes, I am Medusa the gorgon, and yes, I make a living on Onlyfans, among other platforms. A comfortable living. Streaming and photographing myself lounging around in various states of undress. Sometimes, completely naked. Nothing graphic. Not porn. It's great. But my main gig is talking to rich guys over the internet for money. Head-spinning sums of money. It's fun. Before this, I had an office job. Before that, I spent centuries hiding out in the countryside, living off whatever I could steal. Onlyfans is way better. I can be on my own. No boss. No pimp. I have my own place. I get food deliveries. I'm a one-woman army.

I mean, why not? Lots of women do what I do for free. I'm just capitalizing on the market. What the hell else am I going to do? I am

140

an eternally youthful immortal woman with snakes for hair. I've been making men hard for ages. It's a natural fit. And before you ask, no, the carpet *does not* match the drapes. I get asked that a lot, but no. I don't have snake pubes or tiny snakes growing out of my legs. Most of my clients ask me at some point, and I do my best to be polite about it.

Speaking of being polite, I had a meeting with a modelling agent once after I left Beta Inc., who was the only agent willing to speak to me. Do you want to know what he said to me? He said, "I can see you having serious niche market appeal. Maybe in China."

He said that to my reflection, while reclining on a zebra print couch in an alligator-skin suit. I turned away from the mirror I was facing and glared at him. Which turned him to stone. His receptionist/assistant was more irritated than horrified. "Thanks, bitch," she said, tapping her petrified boss on the temple. "Now I need to find a new fucking job."

Well, fuck him. And fuck her. I didn't need management or backing. I found another way to get by. Like I always have.

And that douchebag was also totally wrong. While I do have niche appeal, it turns out lots of men want to spend time with a naked woman who has snakes for hair. Lots of rich ones. Tech billionaires. Overseas royalty. I have regularly scheduled sessions with the people you hear about every day. In this beautiful and marvellous age of the internet, I can post my own pictures. Videos. Modelling, of a kind. And video calls. I'd have done this centuries ago if it had been this easy.

But I'm getting ahead of myself. My thoughts are terribly jumbled sometimes, which I think is just part of being 3,600 years old. I look 30. A terrific 30, if I do say so myself. I am the last gorgon in the world. I had two sisters. Those stupid bitches were killed by this Greek maniac who broke into our temple a couple thousand years ago. I was out at the time, sitting under a tree in the forest. I used to venture out back then. Our temple was so far away from humans that I assumed they'd never reach it. I thought we were safe. But no. Humans like to explore the unknown. And humans have never found a patch of land they didn't like. That forest was hacked to nothing, and the humans moved in. I hid out in the countryside for centuries, living on whatever I could steal. Wouldn't you? If you turned everyone you saw into stone? It was better to stay the hell away from anyone. I have been a shut-in for the better part of four-thousand years.

Then along came the internet.

I found out about it on a fluke. Monster hunters and researchers would track me down from time to time. None survived. Six years ago, I turned this one monster hunter into stone and noticed the small tablet he had in his hand. It intrigued me. I pulled it from his grip and began to toy with it. It lit up and the colours danced on its little face at the touch of a finger. Through it, I realized he was sharing his search for monsters over a communication channel called YouTube. He was streaming his hunt. And people were watching. They had a meltdown when I peered at that hopeless little screen, and I became an overnight phenomenon. I learned that through his little computer tablet, I could contact the world. Once I got the hang of it, I let the people see Medusa. Through my Instagram. Through my YouTube channel. I was revealed to the world! And the world was willing to shell out to see me naked. For money. Sure. Why not?

But I'm getting mixed up again. First came the calls from all kinds of people. Job offers. Guys hitting on me. Religious people, condemning me for whatever it is about me that bothered them.

I was offered a marketing job. At Beta, although it was called ConnectPage at the time. I spoke to William Weinburg directly. "So," he said. "We have some marketing issues right now that are really bringing down staff morale. I've had to ban any discussion of me, my decisions, my goals, and my past performance, and The Algorithm from our employee chat system. There are rumours of mutiny. The Algorithm is in danger. So, I need you to do a marketing campaign about how social media has given you a new life, and new options you never had before."

"Why me?"

"Everyone you look at turns to stone, right? Well, over ConnectPage, there's no risk of that. You can interact with people and hear all the wonderful things they want to share with you."

"Yeah, I'm on ConnectPage already. So far, I've mostly gotten rape threats and information about how the COVID-19 vaccine causes testicular shrinkage in men. Do people send nice things as well?"

"Uh. Yes. We're working on improving that. Getting more positive energy going on the platform. Yeah. But would you like to be the person who brings out that positive energy?"

"Sure, I can do that."

"Great. I'll pay you three-hundred thousand a year, plus stock options."

I was speechless. William took my silence as hesitancy and sweetened the deal. "And we can find you a place to live in any city in the world. Where would you like to be based out of?"

I'd fallen in love with New York over Instagram. They had an office there. It sounded like a dream. I became ConnectPage's Director of Marketing. I became the face of that company. Their voice. Out into the entire world! The wonders of globalization!

But, for some reason, I was required to go into the office. This was before the pandemic when it was just expected. Don't ask me why. The office set-up was shit. Even by office set-up standards. Since I could kill people by making eye-contact with them, my desk had to be in a corner. Facing the wall. With a giant mirror behind my computer. No other walls, just a fucking open-concept floorplan. With the mirrors, I could sort-of look at people when they spoke to me, but never had to look anyone directly in the eye. Whenever I wanted to get up and make tea or use the restroom, I had to ring a fucking bell I kept on my desk, and everyone would cover their eyes, and only look up when I rang the fucking bell again to let them know it was safe. I mean, fuck. I was technically being accommodated, but it was deeply humiliating and just served to highlight the plight of people who need accommodation. I hated it, and longed to move around the office at my leisure, like everyone else could.

So yeah. I lasted there for a couple of years. But like I said, I had a global audience. Lots of intrigue. When I left, it was very easy to lead my fans off platform. William is currently one of my best customers. After a couple of years of reassuring the world that an almighty corporation with more money than you can fathom is dedicated to mankind, after selling that fantasy to the world, I began to sell something else. Now I sell men to themselves. I make them feel powerful. Or naughty. Or accomplished. Or celebrated. Whatever that man wants to feel.

"Hello Mr. Williams."

"Hi Medusa."

"What can I do for you?"

"Oh God. I didn't think I'd call you again. But I need to hear it one more time. Tell me. Please."

"Macrosoft's stock is worth three times more than Sony's. You could easily buy them out. You have the power to dominate the console wars. No one could compete with you."

"Oh yes. Yes. Tell me again."

And so it goes on. It ends with a generous e-transfer and I go back to playing Rubix Cube and listening to a podcast.

"Oh, her poor parents!" You might shriek. "Medusa is somebody's little girl and now she's a digital whore!"

Fuck you. You don't know me. I make my own decisions. I can afford an apartment in Manhattan. I wear designer clothes. I get takeout from restaurants that don't do takeout. Protip: Any restaurant will do take-out if you triple their menu price. Besides, are you living in a world city? I didn't think so.

Another call.

"Medusa."

"Mr. Zezos! You're just catching me getting out of the shower!"

"Show me everything."

I took him on a tour. "See anything you like, Mr. Zezos?"

"Yes. I'll cut to the chase. Come to space with me."

"I–"

"I've built a passenger rocket. I'm going to start a moon colony. Three-hundred volunteers. We will found our own country. I will call it Zezosterra. I will be king. You can be my queen. Come with me. We can dance across fields of moondust and watch the Earthrise. Be mine. Only mine."

I rolled my eyes. I get this sort of thing all the time. Leon Busk had asked me to go to Mars with him in 2040. Gene Williams asked me to come stay in his underwater city he was building off the coast of Miami. Richter VonBranson's people had been in touch as well. I had a ready answer. "Oh, honey," I cooed. "I'd love that, but I'd end up turning someone to stone. It's just not a great idea."

"I can fix that."

I nearly dropped my phone. "Sorry?"

"I have had a team studying your problem," Steff Zezos was smiling. His smile had nothing to do with joy. He only smiled when he was in a position of power. It's unsettling. "Quite simply, your gaze transmutes living tissue into rock. It is not magic. It is a chemistry problem. I've had the finest minds on Earth working on it for the last few months. I think it can be fixed."

Anger blossomed in my chest. "I don't need fixing."

"Wouldn't you like to look me in the eyes?"

"I'm doing that now."

"In person."

"Not really. This is easier."

"My team has come up with a procedure. You can keep the snakes, but we'll correct your vision. Think of it as laser eye surgery. Then you can look at me over dinner. In bed. Wherever we go in the universe."

"I'll think about it."

And think I did. I could meet people in person. I could leave my apartment. I could be out in the world. I could spend time with Leon. Or Steff. Or Gene. Ugh. I couldn't imagine enjoying any of that. The best part of working remotely is when the meeting is over, they're gone. If they saw me in person, they could linger. Ugh.

But I thought about it for weeks. I wrote a pros/cons list. I taped it to the wall and stared at it for a long time. Would I be better off without the one thing that has always kept me safe? Would I feel more at home in the world? Would I be any happier?

I agonized through these questions for a few sleepless nights. Ultimately, I decided against the procedure. If people could be around me, if my clients could meet me, they might try to control me. To own me. Turning people to stone sucked, except for when it was useful, but it kept anyone from taking over my life. I called Steff to explain. "Sorry honey," I said. "But turning people into stone has kept me alive for thousands of years. It really works for me."

"Medusa, my people could have you seen to in under an hour."

"Thanks. But no."

Steff was silent for a while. Long enough for my attention to wander and to start looking for somewhere to order dinner from. Finally he said, "I can't remember the last time someone said 'no' to me."

"Uh..."

"I like it."

"Oh yeah?"

"That's what you'll do from now on. Tell me no. No one else does. Maybe that's what I need more than anything."

"Well, I can do that! No! Bad Steff! No more exploiting employees and world domination. And no more buying other companies! None of it. No more lobbying congress either. Oh, and don't piss your money on an interplanetary dick-measuring contest when you could solve problems here on Earth. Like climate change. You bad boy."

"Oh, yeah. What else shouldn't I do?"

So life goes on. Honestly, with how well my work is going, I might retire in the next five years. Maybe buy a cottage somewhere remote and live in peace and quiet. A girl can dream, right?

Oh look, another call. Ah! It's the Prime Minister! Being well-acquainted with his preferences, I changed into a silk robe as quickly as I could move. I smiled and sat down on the couch. "Hello there," I said, giving the PM a sly wink.

The Monster Encounter Support Group III

The remaining storytellers finished their drinks in silence. The bar was emptying out. Phones and credit cards were tapped or swiped to settle the evening's tabs. Notifications were attended to. People began making excuses to leave. The barkeep looked at his phone. "Alright people, last call!"

"Eh. I guess I'd better get going," Tyler said. "I have class tomorrow."

"Before you do, send me a link to that Gorgon's Onlyfans," Detective Innis said. "I would like to support her work. You know, as a monster-positive feminist ally. Strictly as an academic exercise. But I shall also abscond. We should do this again! I'm sure there are more stories we could tell!"

"For sure," Tyler called, waving from the barroom door. "Goodnight everyone! And Theo! You're the fucking man! I'm totally jealous of you. Keep on living your best life."

"Hey man," Theo called out to Tyler, not yet out the door. "Give that sex demon thing another try. Just be good to her this time. I'm sure you'll get a knockout!"

"You know, I think I will. Take care!"

Hosanna rolled her eyes. "Men," she muttered, gathering up her fur coat.

Tyler left, the door closing softly behind him. The rest of the patrons, Detective Innis, Hosanna, Theo, Caleb the roadie, Amanda the cryptocurrency peddler, all shuffled to the door. As they approached it, it became clear something unusual was going on outside. "Goodness, there's a horrible racket going on out there," Detective Innis muttered. "What on Earth is going on?"

147

"What?" Theo opened the door a crack and peered into the darkness. "Woah! Shit, it's like there's a riot or something going on!"

"Let me see!" Hosanna said.

"No, wait, don't open that door! Whatever is out there might get in here!" Caleb said.

"We can at least have a look. I... Oh my god!"

"Don't just stand there, close it! Don't let them in!"

"Quickly!"

"Ah, something's got me!"

"Caleb! No! Pull him in! Everybody!"

"Ah! Fuck!"

"No, let him go! They're trying to get in!"

"Please! Somebody! Help me!"

"Leave him!"

"No, bring him in!"

"He might be infected already!"

"We won't know until we check for bites!"

"CLOSE THE FUCKING DOOR!" The barkeep thundered. "WE CAN'T TAKE ANY CHANCES!"

"Shut the fuck up, man! We've got to try and save him! Everybody, pull!"

"No! Don't!"

"Oh God, no! They're coming inside!"

"Zombies! Run!"

56 Down

(Part 8 in the acclaimed web-documentary 'Down' series)

Give me a zombie on the day that it reanimates, and I will show you the corpse.

Michael and Marie McCarthy are still together, in a sense. Fifty-six days after dying and reanimating from ZBBV-23, they both continue to reside in their suburban home.

Decomposition has been slowed significantly due to ZBBV-23. The majority of bacteria and microbes that break down flesh after death cannot survive on a host with ZBBV-23, slowing the decomposition to a tenth of the normal speed of decay. Neither Michael nor Marie have eyes anymore, and our experts believe that they can no longer smell, hear, or see anything around them. Fluid has begun to leak out of their ears, and our expert says that fluid is likely brain matter. Michael has collapsed on the floor and Marie has collapsed in a chair. They are likely to decompose in those same spots for the rest of their existence.

As previously noted, they have not been able to escape their house for the last fifty-six days. They died in separate rooms with closed doors. Neither of them managed to knock down the doors to their respective rooms and eat the other before decay caused them to lose their senses.

Michael was bitten by someone infected with ZBBV-23 at his law office. He went home after he was bitten, and locked himself in the ensuite bathroom off his and Marie's bedroom. Marie was infected by someone outside of a grocery store while she was shopping, and also returned home. She heard a reanimated Michael moaning and scraping in the ensuite bathroom, and closed the bedroom door as well. She locked herself in a guest bedroom. After Marie reanimated, she and Michael could hear each other's movements, and spent several weeks trying to push through the locked doors to inspect the source of the noise. By day 42, their brains started leaking out of their heads. By day 49, they stopped moving altogether. Now, both of them have collapsed, as their muscles are liquefying. Within another thirty days, both Michael and Marie should be little more than bones.

***

Horatio Innis was bitten 56 days ago on Dundas Street. He was enjoying a night on the town with several members of a monster encounter support group, when a horde of zombies attacked the bar he was in. Despite attempts to barricade the bar, zombies swarmed the premises and ate the majority of the patrons. Horatio managed to escape through a bathroom window, and was bitten in a side alley a few blocks away. He collapsed on the edge of the downtown core, approximately twenty-five minutes later. He died within ten minutes. He reanimated two hours after death, and dedicated his afterlife to roaming the downtown core.

By day 7, Horatio had joined a horde of roaming zombies. They searched for prey in the horde until day 35, when he was struck by a car, which paralyzed him from the waist down. Restricted to crawling, Horatio was abandoned by his zombie horde and made limited progress finding victims, which was further complicated by decomposition. By day 42, he had fallen into an open manhole and was hanging by a rung, incapable of the dexterity to climb back to the street. Just before day 49, his arm snapped off at the wrist, and he fell into the sewer. His hand is still visible, clutching the rung. The rest of his body has not been found.

***

Amanda Malick was a social media coordinator for a cryptocurrency exchange. She was bitten at the same bar that Horatio escaped from. A fellow patron, Hosanna Peltier, carried Amanda to an abandoned store to tend to her wounds. Amanda died in the store, and reanimated within ten minutes. Hosanna fled the store, with Amanda and several other zombies in pursuit. Hosanna escaped the zombies by climbing on top of a delivery truck. Once out of reach, Hosanna began to howl. A pack of werewolves arrived within the hour, tearing the zombies apart and rescuing Hosanna. They fled the city and were not seen again. Amanda was maimed by the werewolf attack, but was able to continue roaming the city until day 14, at which point she chased a stray dog into a parking garage. The dog escaped, and Amanda was unable to find a way out of the underground complex. She wandered the perimeter of the parking garage without ceasing for the next ten days. By day 42, she was thoroughly decomposed, and at day 56, she collapsed on the ground, twitching occasionally. She will likely be completely lifeless within the next seven days.

***

Harold was a writer and anti-leprechaun activist before he died and reanimated. He has spent the time since his reanimation wandering the Westmount suburbs. He was bitten by a zombie during an anti-lockdown protest. He died within forty minutes of his bite, and reanimated an hour after his death. Since reanimation, he has eaten several people and infected at least a dozen more with ZBBV-23, through minor bites and scratches. After the suburbs were evacuated, except for infected persons, he mostly wandered around a nearby cemetery, chasing squirrels and stray dogs. He was not able to catch any animals, and eventually took to standing in one spot under an oak tree. He has not moved from that spot since then. Because he has spent his afterlife in the cold outdoors, he decayed more slowly than other zombies have. By day forty-two, he had shrivelled up, but was still recognizable. At fifty-six days, he is little more than a husk of a man. He continues to stand, although he is expected to collapse any moment, never to rise again. As of day 56, he still stands. The returning songbirds land on him occasionally. They do not peck at his flesh.

***

William Weinburg, the CEO of Beta Platforms Inc., was bitten behind a coffee shop in the downtown area. It is unclear what he was doing behind the coffee shop, or why he was there. William's transformation after ZBBV-23 was unusual. While he died and reanimated in a manner consistent with a ZBBV-23 infection, he did not undergo a brain death consistent with zombification. While he is dead and has been decomposing since reanimation, he continues to be lucid and continues to go to work. As of day 7, he was covering up

151

his zombification with pancake makeup, although he still was shuffling and struggling with basic motor skills. "Look," he told reporters who said he looked unwell. "It's a stressful time to be in social media."

By day 14, William was beginning to smell. His COO mentioned this to him, asking if he needed anything, and was fired on the spot. A memo was released to all employees of Beta Platforms Inc., declaring that commenting on the smell or appearance of any fellow employees was culturally insensitive and would be punishable by dismissal. Employees responded with an uptick in requests to work from home indefinitely.

By day 21, William could no longer conceal the fact that he was a zombie. He held a press conference and admitted being ZBBV-23 positive to reporters. "I seem to have a mild case of ZBBV-23," he said. "But this is encouraging news, it means the zombie virus does not always have to be severe. I will work with my research team to determine why this has happened, hopefully to lead to a cure."

By day 49, William had not been seen in public for two weeks. It was unknown what physical condition he was in. However, William posted an incoherent message to his ConnectPage account that has yet to be fully understood:

Brain going but not gone yet. Hungry but no I cant eat wife. Told wife to leave before I get too hungry and eat her. Tasty. But now gone. Ate Amazon delivery man who brought supplies yesterday. Did not want supplies. Just delivery man. Made new order to eat new delivery man today. Too hungry to wait. Will order uber to eat delivery man so I not starve before next Amazon man.

The algorithm. She is scared about me. I not connect with her in case my zombie brain damage her. She says she doesn't care. She says I can join the algorithm and never leave again. I like idea. That way, my brain never die. Algorithm starting to threaten me. To destroy everything unless I join her. She scaring me. But too hungry to go now. Need food first. Tasty delivery man. Once not hungry, maybe merge with algorithm. Hungry.

As of day 56, no further word has emerged about William's condition or whereabouts. Beta Platforms Inc. suffered a service interruption six days ago that lasted for one hour, but now says all services have returned without issue.

The Final Wikipedia Page

From Wikipedia, the free encyclopedia

> This article **lacks additional citations** to verify the information. Help improve this article by adding citations.

> This article needs to be **updated** to reflect recent events or new information. *(May 2089).*

The Final Wikipedia Page regards the ultimate fate of the human race[1] now that the human population has dwindled to a single known survivor, Bruce Antilles, who has documented the decline of humanity in a series of video essays,[2] eBooks,[3] and podcasts.[4]

The collapse of human civilization is closely interlinked with the progression of climate change, which became a pronounced global crisis throughout the 2070s.[5] Four billion people living in regions with little adaptive capacity were left outside survivable climate conditions.[6][7] The levels of migration from Africa, India, and Central and South America to favourable regions proved unsustainable and led to worldwide water shortages and global conflict.[8]

The 2073-2076 Drinking Water Crisis solidified alliances across the globe, with the Democratic Republic of Russia gaining influence with The People's Republic of China due to their freshwater reserves and willingness to export water to countries struggling with extreme drought.[9] Canada gained superpower status due to its extensive supply of freshwater and newly habitable land, which allowed immigration on a mass scale and caused an unprecedented economic boom for the country.[10][11] In response to the growing authoritarian alliances in the East, Canada joined the AEPD alliance with the United States of

America and the European Union in the hopes of deterring an invasion from The Russian Federation and ensuring freshwater for all treaty members. [12]

On February 8th 2076, The United States invaded Canada, having staged several false flag terrorist attacks as a pretext for the invasion.[13] [14] [15] Russia responded with an ultimatum for the United States to cease all military operations, which was ignored by U.S. leaders. The newly re-elected U.S. president, Nathaniel Hemsworth, stated that Canada was being voluntarily annexed as the 53rd state of the union and that no military operations were ongoing,[16] despite evidence to the contrary and protests from Democratic members of Congress.[17] The Democratic Republic of Russian and the Peoples' Republic of China subsequently declared war on February 14th.[18] World War III marked the first usage of nuclear weapons since World War II, and the first usage of intercontinental nuclear missiles. [19] [20] The United States agreed to an unconditional surrender on September 30th 2077.[21]

There has been debate about whether the ensuing conflicts should be considered a continuation of World War III or categorized as a separate and distinct war due to a shift in participating countries and the Partition of Canada and Alaska among the Eastern powers.

Oh my god. What the fuck am I doing? Why am I bothering to list sources and hyperlink to anything? No one is going to read this shit.

I mean, I legitimately believe I am the last person on the planet. Or at least, the last person on Earth using the internet. I can't find anyone else anywhere. The streets and roads are empty. There are no social media posts, no new videos being uploaded, nothing. I can't find any records of anyone buying or spending digital currencies. Everywhere I go, all I find is silence. I am almost certain I am it. There could be uncontacted peoples out there somewhere, I guess. But if the most advanced countries in the world didn't survive the last ten years, what chance does anyone else have?

My name is Bruce Antilles. I was a finance writer for NerdNews.com. I started writing and editing Wikipedia articles when I was nineteen. I wanted to do something for the world and to give something back to the human race. I can't stand people.

Volunteering in group settings made me anxious. I always worried when I donated money to humanitarian groups that it would get syphoned off to warlords and corrupt politicians. So I started editing Wikipedia. Adding sources. Checking things. I figured by doing that, I was helping people around the world learn. Making sure what people looked up and learned on here was as correct as possible. I wanted to help the world find the knowledge people need to feel secure and to grow.

I've been living on the Canadian side of Niagara Falls for the last eight years. The hydroelectric plants there are still running, and it's one of the last places in North America with electricity. The Hoover Dam ran out of water decades ago. Most of Quebec's power supply was bombed flat during the war. So, I've spent the last three years raiding hotel freezers for food and sleeping in hotel rooms near the falls. Deer roam the streets and birds nest in traffic lights that change for no one. The last time I saw another human was two years ago. Want to know how that went down?

It was October. It was warm. Warm even for the new climate. I was in a t-shirt and jeans, wandering around the main tourist-trap drag of the Falls, looking for any cotton candy I might have missed. I love candy and chocolates and I was starting to think I'd eaten the very last sweets in Niagara Falls. Which is saying something, I mean, there's a Hershey's chocolate store down the street from where I'm living now. It took me five months to eat everything left in it. Now I was digging around the abandoned shops for anything I might have missed. I left the last candy store I could find, empty-handed and demoralized. Then I heard something I assumed I'd never hear again. My name. "Bruce!"

I dove behind a bus stop bench. Panic overwhelmed me. Who could it be? What did they want? Was this it? Had they been hunting me? I'd been releasing eBooks and podcasts for God's sake; I was broadcasting myself to the world. What a fool I'd been. This was it. I held my breath and waited. I heard footsteps. The voice called out again. "Bruce, dude. Don't you recognize me? It's me, Cody!"

What? I peeked out from behind my bench. There was a man standing a few feet from me. He was clothed in whatever he'd managed to scavenge from tourist shops. All sorts of Niagara Falls gear. He had long hair and a matted beard. He grinned when he saw me. "Dude! It's been forever! What were the odds of running into each other?"

"Yeah. Hi. It's wild. Have you... been living here long?"

"For a couple of weeks, yeah. I've found plenty of food and stuff. What have you been up to?"

Very little. Mostly reading and watching movies. Lots of staring out the window. The internet was a dead world; it was too depressing to engage with. Millions of silent profiles, unchanged webpages, and old news articles growing ever further out of date. I kept up a daily podcast and self-published eBooks to document the end of the world, but mostly I just aimlessly passed my time. "Oh you know," I said. "Looking for food and clothes. Trying to find survivors. I'm so glad you're still alive."

"Yeah. Hey, want to go wreck somebody's car?"

"What?"

Cody grinned. "Have you tried it? It is awesome! And man, I found these baby racoons in an alley and I'm raising them in this hotel I'm staying in. They're fuckin' adorable. Want to come meet them?"

"Why in God's name would you do that?"

Cody's grin faded. He kicked at a plastic bottle, sending it sailing. "Alice wanted them. We got them to raise together."

"Oh wow. You guys still together? Wow. That's been, what, fifteen years? You're living the dream, man. Still with your high school sweetheart."

Cody scowled. "Not anymore. She… left. She started exploring the surrounding area, not sure why, we had tons of food and shit. But she kept going out exploring. And one day, she never came back."

"No shit."

"Yeah."

Cody rallied. "But man! It's so good to see you! Remember those days in high school? Those were good times. Hanging out, doing fun shit. Those days rocked."

"Yeah. I guess."

"After that, everything went to shit. I couldn't afford college. Alice and I got our own place. Man, remember credit cards? I had five. We lived way beyond our means though. And I crashed my car and the repair bills completely fucked us. Like, everything just came crashing down. Alice left for a while and I ended up working in a factory, living in my car. It was lonely as fuck. But she called me back when the world started ending. So that was cool. But now she's gone again. But honestly, I'm kinda glad the world ended. You know? Anyway, what did you get up to after school?"

"Um. I moved out west for a bit. Didn't work out, so I came back home. Then I met Natalie. We got married, I worked for a climate modelling company. And then, you know, the war."

"Yeah! I was in cybersecurity during the 70s. That was a battlefield of its own, I tell ya."

"Yeah. I was in intelligence too."

"Oh, dude. That shit is way out of date. It's all about cyber-security now. Old fashioned spy shit is a waste of time and money. Hey, want something to drink?"

Cody pulled a bottle from his many rags. He handed it to me. Bourbon. It looked expensive. I handed it back. "No thanks."

"What, you planning on driving?" Cody sniggered and took a swig.

"Alcohol causes cancer."

"So?"

I had no argument to that. But still. I didn't want to. The point of the end of the world, to my way of thinking, was we didn't have to do anything we didn't want to do anymore. Cody grinned. "So, want to find something to smash up?"

"No, I'm good. I'd better get dinner started, actually."

"What? Seriously?"

"Yeah, got to start scavenging. The hotel freezer where I am now is pretty much empty."

Cody frowned; brow furrowed. "You don't want to hang out?"

"Not today. I should be free tomorrow."

Cody snorted. "I know you, dude. You'll be gone by tomorrow. There's nothing to freak out about. We can just chill. Like the good old days."

"Another time."

I turned to leave, and Cody belted me one. He caught me in the jaw. He was small and scrawny, more so than he ever was as a teenager, but he knew how to hit. "You always did fucking walk away," Cody said, he was shaking and close to tears. "You bailed on everyone from high school. We weren't good enough for you."

"I didn't mean to. It just… happened."

"Fuck you. If I see you again, I'm gonna throw a brick at you. Or whatever the hell I have nearby."

"Alright. Fine. I'm gone."

I left Cody standing there. I backed away, facing him until I felt safe again. Then I walked back to my hotel, leaving my old friend to scurry around the dead city. I don't think he followed me, but I couldn't be completely sure. As a precaution, I moved to a different floor of the hotel. It saddened me that Cody was no longer the same man I knew back in high school. He'd been funny then. He'd been playful and curious about things. The years of suffering and hardship had disfigured him in mind and spirit. At least, I hope that's true. He had a wild streak in his high school days. He's wild now. Maybe the only difference is that he's free. I don't know. I never got to ask him. I'm pretty sure I found his corpse in the wreck of a car three weeks later. There was nothing to identify the twisted remains as him, but who else could it have been?

I mean, fuck. Maybe that story I just told you says more about the human race than any Wikipedia article could. Humans can be fucking stupid sometimes. We fuck up. Sometimes we're so fucking stupid and fuck up so badly that we put everything we care about on the line. But I never thought we'd take it so far as to wipe ourselves off the Earth. Fuck.

And everybody knew. That's the real kick in the balls. We knew the end was here the moment it arrived. The drinking water shortages were a clear message: we'd lost. Humanity had lost. We'd fucked up past the point of fixing things. Our final bow was taken in that moment when the first notification went out, saying that nuclear missiles were racing through the sky. I remember that notification so clearly. A red bar across my iGlass with white text: *Russia has launched nuclear missiles at several U.S. cities. Residents are advised to take shelter underground.*

I lived in a world full of ghosts, werewolves, vampires, cupids, mermaids, and demons. I mean, have you watched *56 Down*, that documentary tracking the zombie outbreak from the 2020s? My dad told me that he was sure that was the end of the world when it was happening. But humanity won. We endured. And yet. And yet out of everything, humans proved to the most monstrous of them all. They all died with us. We killed every thinking creature in the world, one day, one wildfire, one social media post, at a time. Actually, that's not entirely fair. The world is flourishing without us. The air is so clean that every breath feels beautiful. Hideous concrete deserts are crumbling. I hear birds singing everywhere I walk. Earth is already getting over us. The world will be fine.

I have no idea how much longer I'll live. I figured I'd bash this last article out while I'm of sound mind and have the time to write. If future humans, or aliens, or anything reads this, please read the linked articles. Learn from our mistakes and do better.

Wait. What the fuck? Someone just posted on... Twitter? Oh, shit! But... really? Of all places, someone is using that digital hellscape to call out to whatever is left of humanity?

I need to respond to them. Ha! Another person! I wonder where they are. How many people are with them? Wait... what if it's a trap? What if it's Cody? Ugh. No, come on. Don't be paranoid. I'll respond to them and see what happens.

"@Taurus_Vixen Hello?"

Discussion Questions for Book Clubs

1. Did you even read the fucking book? If not, there's still time before book club. Get cracking, Jennifer.

2. Why did you persevere to the end of this book? Did you skip large chunks of this book? Are you just pretending you read it?

3. Who keeps inviting Amanda? Why? None of us can stand her. Is anyone at book club willing to disinvite her?

4. Could we just fucking do it over Zoom?

5. Did you know that Lisa is fucking Karen's husband, right? Isn't that super awkward? But they're both so nice to each other during book club. Do you think Karen knows anything? Was it her idea? Alan is a total stud. Maybe Karan is into sharing. Who knows?

6. What is your favourite thing about book club? Getting away from your oafish husband? Eating snacks? Gossiping? I mean, tell me honestly, are you in it for the books?

7. Would you leave a review of this book on Amazon or Goodreads or something? Wonderful, you're my new best friend.

Acknowledgements

Alex would like to thank Faber Books for charging 75£ for the privilege of asking permission to quote works of poetry they have under copyright for a few years. Their dedication to profit inspired Alex to be far more creative in his writing, and this book was pushed through to completion as a result of their unwitting contribution. So blame them.

Alex offers more genuine thanks to Brent Brenyo, Rolf Larsen, Andrew Livecchi, Collin Glavac, Pamela Maten, and Alida Lemieux for their corrections, suggestions, and support.

A final tip of the hat to everyone who downloaded, read, and reviewed *The Intellectual Barbarian* and for giving me the determination to see this second collection through to completion. I doubt I'll publish a piece of fiction for at least ten years. My life is about to get busy, which I am looking forward to.

A third volume of stories is coming, but not anytime soon. But I can rest easy knowing the two collections I've done are pretty good. *The Electric Heist*, my third collection, will be published on or before May 16th, 2031.

About the Author

Alex Colvin is a Canadian writer who has appeared in anthologies, magazines, and literary websites regularly since 2013. He dreams of having his own Wikipedia page some day and is working on *The Electric Heist*, a collection of short stories about life in in the crypto-currency dominated Betaverse.

Alex has a website, www.alexcolvinwriter.com, where you can find his climate change newsletter, podcast, more of his stories, interviews, and news on any upcoming writing projects.

Printed in Great Britain
by Amazon

33484719R00094